Passion SO
2038
HARLEQUIN ®

EMMA DARCY

The Secret Mistress

HARLEQUIN®
Makes any time special ™

AVAILABLE THIS MONTH:

"What do you want from me, Luis?"

"What I had before."

Shontelle's mind fragmented under the force of his apparent desire to repeat the passion they'd shared. Some tattered shreds of reason shrieked that he was only playing with her.

"What do you mean?" she cried.

"I mean to seize the day, Shontelle. Or, to put it more graphically...*the night*. I want one more taste of you."

Shock waves slammed through her. *One more taste....* Only *one....*

"Not such a difficult deal, is it?" Luis taunted. "Just a matter of giving me what you gave of yourself two years ago...in your desire to get what you wanted of me."

"I didn't get what I wanted then," she protested, her voice thin and shaky under the appalling weight of devastated hopes.

A savage fury flared into his eyes. "Was I not all you wanted of a Latin lover?" His mouth curled with cruel intent. "Well, let me try not to disappoint you tonight."

EMMA DARCY

The Secret Mistress

Passion™

HARLEQUIN®

TORONTO • NEW YORK • LONDON
AMSTERDAM • PARIS • SYDNEY • HAMBURG
STOCKHOLM • ATHENS • TOKYO • MILAN • MADRID
PRAGUE • WARSAW • BUDAPEST • AUCKLAND

To Lew Pulbrook, whose INCA TOURS of
South America inspired this book and provided all of
the background material in it. Many, many thanks to
Lew and Kristy for sharing their knowledge and
experience, while showing me and all "The Amigos"
a fantastic and fascinating part of the world.

ISBN 0-373-12038-9

THE SECRET MISTRESS

First North American Publication 1999.

Look us up on-line at: http://www.romance.net

Printed in U.S.A.

CHAPTER ONE

LUIS ANGEL MARTINEZ was feeling good as he rode the elevator up to his hotel suite. He'd completed the business he'd come to La Paz to do, he'd dined well, the current crisis in the city provided him with the perfect excuse for missing his own engagement party, and his mother—widely regarded as the wealthiest and most powerful woman in Argentina—couldn't do one damned thing about it.

He couldn't help smiling.

The two young women who were sharing the elevator—their accents and clothes marking them as tourists from the U.S.A.—turned interested, hopefully inviting eyes on him. Luis instantly killed the smile. Black scorn blazed from his dark eyes, shrivelling their speculation, and his whole body stiffened in proud rejection of whatever fantasies they nursed.

He despised the foreign women who tripped around, looking for sexual adventure, and he most particularly hated being viewed as a possible Latin lover. He might look the part, having the dark olive skin and black hair of his Spanish heritage, with the added attraction of a taller, more powerful physique than the average South American male, but he sure as hell would never get drawn into playing the part.

5

He'd been burnt once. Once was more than enough for him.

The elevator halted. He glared balefully at the back of the two blonde heads as the women made their exit. Not that their fairness compared in any way to the silky sun and moon mixture of Shontelle's hair, but the minds under the hair probably held the same attitude towards sampling one of the natives for the pleasure of a new carnal experience.

Not me, ladies, he savagely beamed at them before the doors shut and the elevator resumed its upward climb. His mother was right on one score. Best to tie himself to a woman of his own race, own culture, own background. No nasty surprises with that kind of matchmaking. All smooth sailing. Especially with Elvira Rosa Martinez at the helm, steering everything as she saw fit.

Except she hadn't counted on this little squall blowing up in Bolivia, causing him to miss the engagement party she had planned behind his back.

Unavoidable circumstances.

The absolutely perfect excuse.

The thought restored Luis' good humour. He was smiling again as the elevator opened onto his floor and he headed for his private suite. No one could validly question his staying right here. It was literally impossible for him to get out of La Paz without running into trouble.

After yesterday's violent march of the farmers through the streets, Bolivia was boiling up to yet another change of government. The airport was closed. A curfew had been imposed. The military had taken over the city.

Safely and comfortably ensconced in the Plaza Hotel, Luis was not in the least perturbed by these events. Bolivia was Bolivia, renowned for having more changes of government than any other country, five in one day in recent history. The volatile political situation would eventually blow over and life would go on as usual.

He entered his well-appointed suite, closed the door on all the outside problems, and moved to the mini-bar, deciding one or two more celebratory drinks were in order.

Of course, a second engagement party would be arranged, although he'd insist on doing it himself—*his* way—next time. This minor reprieve was only a postponement of the inevitable. He was thirty-six years old, time for him to marry, time for him to start a family. It was also time for his mother to step right out of his affairs.

She'd undoubtedly be stewing with frustration over this further delay to a public announcement of her most cherished ambition—the tying of the Martinez fortune to that of the Gallardo family. Do her good, Luis thought with intense satisfaction. She was far too fond of pushing.

She'd picked Claudia Gallardo out for him very shortly after his brother's death. Luis had scoffed at the idea—a schoolgirl! She'd be groomed to suit him,

to grace their social position, to uphold all the traditional virtues of a wife, his mother had argued. I'll
choose my own wife, he'd tossed back at her at the
time, but he really didn't care anymore, not since
Shontelle—that green-eyed witch—had chewed him
up and spat him out.

He took ice and a lime from the refrigerator, lined
up the bottle of *Caipirinha,* and wished he could blot
the memory of Shontelle Wright right out of existence. Because of her…after her…he'd wanted more
than just a *suitable* wife. He'd wanted to feel…

But maybe he didn't have any passion left in him,
so what did it matter if his marriage bed wasn't as
warm as he'd like it? Stupid to keep holding out for
something he might never experience again. He
would make the commitment to Claudia soon enough.
She was willing. He was willing. Together they'd be-
get another line of heirs and heiresses. Surely he'd
feel something for his children.

Nevertheless, it was one thing resigning himself to
the destiny mapped out for him, another to be relentlessly pressed into it. Although he'd finally put his
rebellious years behind him and shouldered the
responsibilities that would have been his older
brother's, had Eduardo lived, Luis did not want his
mother thinking she could rule his life. He was glad—
yes, glad—he couldn't fly back to Buenos Aires to
keep *her* timetable, however *reasonable* it was.

Claudia would undoubtedly wait submissively.

She did everything…submissively.

Luis grimaced. Sometimes he suspected it was an act, deliberately put on to give him the sense of being on top. Respected. Honoured. King of his kingdom. But, so what? At least he knew where he was with Claudia.

He dropped the wedges of lime into his glass, mashed sugar into them, added the ice and drowned the lot with *Caipirinha.* Sweet and sour—like life, he thought. The telephone rang as he stirred the drink. Carrying the glass with him, he moved to pick up the nearest receiver, cynically wondering if his mother had found a danger-free way out of La Paz for him.

"Luis Martinez," he rolled out carelessly.

"Luis, it's Alan Wright. Please...don't hang up. It's taken me hours to track you down and I desperately need your help."

The quick, taut plea stilled what would normally have been an automatic reaction. Luis had no wish to see, hear, or have any contact with the man whose sister had taken him for no more than a lump of tasty Latin meat. The heat of deeply lacerated pride instantly burned through him.

"What kind of help?" he snapped, angry with himself for even hesitating over cutting off his former friend.

"Luis, I have a tour group caught here in La Paz. We were due to fly to Buenos Aires yesterday. God knows when the airport will be reopened. They're frightened, panicky, and some are suffering from altitude sickness. I need a bus to get them out. I'll drive it. I thought you might be able to provide it.''

A bus.

It conjured up old memories—a much younger, wilder Alan, driving a beaten-up bus through the Amazon jungle to the mining operation where Luis had been sent for safekeeping, away from the troubles in Argentina. Alan had worked there for six months, more or less swapping his mechanical skills for the spare parts he needed to get his bus roadworthy enough to set up his own tour business.

An Australian, in love with South America—nothing was going to stop Alan Wright from selling it to tourists back home. Camping trips to start with, he'd decided. Then gradually he'd build up to the bigger money stuff. Luis had admired his initiative and determination, liked his cheerful good nature, and enjoyed his company. For nine years they'd maintained an infrequent but always congenial contact with each other. If Alan hadn't introduced his sister...

"Is Shontelle with you?"

The question slipped out, unconsidered and loaded with a long, pent-up hostility that hissed down the line.

No denial. Nothing but a fraught silence that emphatically underlined the division of their interests.

"Is she?" Luis demanded harshly, uncaring of what the other man thought, knowing he had the power to ruthlessly cut their connection without any comeback.

"Goddammit, Luis! I'll pay you for the bus. Can't you just deal with me?" Alan exploded, tension and urgency ripping through every word.

She was with him.

More than pride started burning through Luis Angel Martinez. Every cell of his body was hit by an electric charge. Adrenalin shot through his bloodstream. Even the sense of his sexuality leapt into powerful prominence...sharply revitalised, wanting, needing, craving the satisfaction of wringing something more from the woman who'd dismissed all they'd shared as a brief bout of lust, come to the end of its run.

"Where are you?" he asked.

"At the Europa Hotel," came the quick, hopeful answer. "As luck would have it, just around the corner from the Plaza."

"Very convenient!" Luis smiled. It was a smile that would have chilled the heart of anyone who saw it. "What's the size of your tour group, Alan?"

"Thirty-two, including me."

"I can get you a suitable bus..."

"Great!" A gush of relief.

"...And have it at your hotel, ready to go in the morning..."

"I knew if anyone could do it, you could." Warm gratitude.

"...On one condition."

Silence. On edge again. "What is it?" Wary.

Luis didn't give a damn about Alan's feelings. His

friendship had probably been as self-serving as his sister's association with him. After all, for a foreign tour operator, Luis Angel Martinez was a contact worth having in South America. He could open doors.

And shut them.

"Shontelle will have to come to my suite at the Plaza to negotiate the deal with me," he stated blandly. "The sooner the better, for your purposes."

"You can't be serious!" Alan burst out. "There's a curfew on. Army tanks are trundling around the streets and trigger-happy soldiers are everywhere. A woman alone, breaking curfew...it's too dangerous, Luis."

So was driving a bus out of here, Luis thought. The farmers were in revolt. They'd be blockading all the roads from La Paz. Alan was obviously prepared to take risks to get his people out, probably counting on his skill as a good talker with a dab hand at appropriate bribery. Which he could use tonight, as well, if need be. His plea on Shontelle's behalf left Luis totally unmoved.

"You can escort her from hotel to hotel, if you like. The distance is very short and the road that links us is a cul-de-sac, hardly the place for a tank or soldiers on guard duty," he pointed out.

"I can't leave the group. Shontelle can't, either. The women need her to..."

"There is a side entrance to the Plaza from the steps leading up to Prado 16 de Julio. I'll have a man posted at the door to let her in. Let's say…half an hour from now?''

Luis set the receiver down with firm decisiveness. He smiled again as he jiggled the ice in his drink. A responsibility to others often led to paths one wouldn't take, given an absolutely free choice. Because he was his mother's son, he would end up married to Claudia Gallardo. Because Shontelle was Alan Wright's sister, she would end up in this suite tonight.

With him.

And he would take a great deal of pleasure in stripping her of more than her clothes!

CHAPTER TWO

SHONTELLE saw her brother's jaw clench. He literally gnashed his teeth as he slammed the telephone receiver down. The violent action caused her heart to leap out of the frozen stasis that had held it for the duration of the call. The resulting pump of blood kicked reason into her mind, clearing it of the dark cloud of memories.

"What did he want?" she asked. It was obvious from the conversation that Luis had at least considered procuring the bus. It was certainly possible for him to do so. The Martinez family had fingers in many pies right across the continent; agriculture, mining, cement works, oil and gas, transport...

"Forget it!" Alan's hand sliced the air with negative vehemence. "I'll try something else."

There was nothing else. Shontelle shook her head over the mess of notes on the table. They'd already been down every other avenue. The usual help Alan could tap into was not forthcoming.

She watched him steam around the sitting room of the suite they were sharing, a big man chopping up the space around her, making it feel claustrophobic with the sense of failure. Getting accommodation in The Europa, a relatively new five-star hotel, had been a coup for this tour. Now it seemed like a prison. Everyone in the tour group had lost their pleasure in its luxury, anxieties building with being trapped here. More bad news could make soothing fears and frayed tempers a very difficult, if not impossible exercise.

Alan always fought against imparting bad news to his tour groups, especially when there was no good news to make it more palatable. Normally he was a very cool operator, highly skilled at lateral thinking whenever a crisis arose, as it frequently did in South America. The ability to be flexible was paramount to bringing off a successful tour and Alan was always prepared to come up with an alternative schedule. But this time he'd found himself blocked at every turn.

He was the kind of man who hated being thwarted.

Or found wanting in any way.

So was Luis Angel Martinez, Shontelle remembered.

The two men were very alike in that respect. Kindred spirits. They'd been friends...the type of friendship where time and distance and social standing had no relevance. They might not meet for long intervals but such separations hadn't made any difference, not over the nine years before...

Guilt wormed through Shontelle.

She had ruined it. For both of them. Blindly, wantonly, foolishly. Alan had warned her it wouldn't work between her and Luis. Couldn't. But she had refused to listen, refused to see...until Elvira Rosa Martinez had so very forcefully opened her ears and eyes. Then she'd been too wrapped up in her pride to realise how her exit from Luis' life might have a bitter fallout on his friendship with her brother.

Not that Alan had told her of the consequences of her decisions. She had overheard Vicki, his wife, dryly informing an office associate they were no longer welcome on Martinez territory. The popular day trip from Buenos Aires to the ranch run by Luis' younger brother, Patricio, had been struck from the tour.

When she'd tackled Vicki about it, the forthcoming explanation had been devastating. "Shontelle, did you really expect Luis Martinez to keep up the connection? You and Alan are not only of the same family, you even look alike."

It was true. Alan was ten years older than her but the family likeness was unmistakable. The bone structure of their faces was the same; wide brow, high cheekbones, straight nose, clearcut chin. Alan's top lip was thinner than hers and his eyes were not a clear green—more hazel in colour. The streaky blonde hair of his youth had darkened over the years but the variation in shade was still there. Either one of them was a physical reminder of the other, and that reminder would not be welcome to Luis Angel Martinez.

In her pride, Shontelle knew she had wounded his. It hadn't seemed to matter at the time. But it did. She had the strong conviction it especially mattered now.

"You were talking to Luis about me," she said, drawing Alan's attention.

He flashed her a pained look. "He asked about you," he answered dismissively.

"No. It was more than that." She frowned, trying to recall what she'd heard. The call had ended abruptly, just after Alan had said it was too dangerous for a woman to be out during curfew. "Tell me what he wanted, Alan."

"I said, forget it!" he snapped impatiently.

"I want to know. I have a right to know," she argued. "I'm just as responsible for this tour group as you are."

He paused in his pacing but aggression still pumped from him. His eyes glittered with a fury of frustration. "I will not have my little sister grovel to Luis Martinez for anyone!" he bit out.

More pride.

It was heart-thumpingly obvious that Luis had turned the deal for the bus into something personal. Very personal. Which again was her fault. Shontelle took a deep breath to calm a host of skittish nerves. She couldn't let this pass. It wasn't fair to Alan. Besides which, the tour group was depending on them to rescue them from the situation.

"I'm not little," she pointed out determinedly. "I'm twenty-six years old and I can take care of myself."

Alan rolled his eyes. "Sure you can! Like you did two years ago when you talked me into leaving you with Luis."

"I'm over that. I can deal with him," she insisted hotly.

Too much personal knowledge sliced back at her. "You didn't want to come back to South America. You wouldn't be on this trip but for Vicki getting glandular fever. And you were as nervy as hell while we were in Buenos Aires."

Her cheeks burned. "I came to assist you. That's my job." She pushed her chair back from the table which was littered with the evidence of failed attempts at solutions. Resolution drove her to her feet. "I'll go and talk to him."

"No, you won't!"

"Luis Martinez was your last resort, Alan. Two years ago he would have got you the bus, no problem. I caused the problem and I'll deal with it."

He argued.

Shontelle stood firm.

Nothing was going to stop her; not the curfew, not the danger—which she considered very limited with the Plaza Hotel being virtually next door—not any of Alan's big-brotherly concerns. She'd lived with guilt and shame too long. She'd spent two years being eaten up by memories she couldn't change or bury. Luis Martinez wanted a face-to-face meeting with her. Then let it be. Let it be.

Maybe something good would come out of it.

The bus, if nothing else.

She owed Alan that.

CHAPTER THREE

GOOD intentions were all very fine when made from a safe distance. Shontelle stared at the door which led into the suite occupied by Luis Angel Martinez and her heart quailed. A suite contained a bed...

She wasn't over him. She doubted she ever would be. Luis Angel... She'd even been besotted with his name. Dark angel, she thought now, barely suppressing a shiver. It took all her willpower to raise her hand and knock on the door.

In the next few stomach-knotting moments, Shontelle tried to steel herself against revealing the vulnerability she felt. This meeting would only be a matter of pride to the man she had to face. He undoubtedly wanted to rub in that she was the loser, not him.

Somehow she had to let that wash over her, do a bit of grovelling if need be. Remember the bus, she fiercely told herself. She had to get the bus.

At least Luis couldn't mistake the fact she was dressed for business. Her dark red T-shirt was printed with the *Amigos Tours* logo and her khaki trousers with pockets running down both legs were plainly practical, as were her sturdy shoes. This was strictly a business visit.

The door opened.

And there he was, hot flesh and blood, simmering in front of her. His thick, wavy black hair was brushed away from the beautifully sculpted features of his face, as always, framing them with a kind of dark, savage splendour. His skin gleamed with almost a magnetic vitality. His deeply set eyes, lushly outlined by their double rows of lashes, projected more power than any one man should ever have.

Shontelle stood rooted to the floor, speechless, breathless, mindless, her good intentions instantly zapped out of existence. Her scalp tingled. Every millimetre of her skin tingled. Her fingers curled into her palms, nails biting into flesh. Her toes scrunched up in her walking boots. Her heart swelled, throbbed, its heavy beat of yearning echoing through every pulse point.

She wanted him.

She still wanted him.

"Welcome back to my part of the world."

His voice jolted her back to the chilling reality of why she was here. She'd loved his voice—its deep, rich, flowing tones—but there was no caress in it now, nothing warmly intimate. No welcome in his smile, either. The full-lipped sensual mouth that had once seduced her with such passion, was curled into a sardonic taunt, and the dark blaze of his eyes held a scorching intensity that shrivelled any hope of reviving good feelings. Or even a workable understanding.

He stepped aside to make room for her to enter,

derisively waving her into his domain. For one nerve-jangling instant, the highly civilised Plaza suite blurred in Shontelle's mind and the Amazon jungle leapt into it—its overwhelming sense of the primitive pressing in on her, vampire bats biting for blood, big black tarantulas hiding in trees, ready to pounce on their prey...

"Scared?" Luis mocked, his eyes raking her with contempt.

It goaded her forward. "No. Should I be?" she tossed at him as she passed by, determined on holding a brave front.

He closed the door behind her.

The metallic click felt ominous.

"Spurned Latin lovers are notoriously volatile," he remarked, still in a mocking tone.

"A lot of water under the bridge since then, Luis," she answered, shrugging off the implied threat and walking on through the sitting room of the suite, aiming for the big picture window on the other side of it.

The spectacular view of La Paz at night was not the drawcard. She desperately needed to put distance between her and the man who'd deliberately raised memories of their affair. And its ending.

"I must say you look as dynamic as ever," she threw at him, forcing herself to attach a conciliatory smile. "I'd say life has been treating you well."

"It could be better," he replied, watching her move

away from him with a dark amusement that raised Shontelle's sense of danger several notches.

"I expect you're married by now," she added, trying to drive a moral wedge between them.

His white shirt was half unbuttoned, revealing a provocative arrowhead of his broad muscular chest, dark skin tipped by a glimpse of the black curls she knew spread across it. His forearms were bare, too, sleeves rolled up, flaunting his strong masculinity. She hated the thought of his wife knowing him as intimately as she had.

"No. As it happens, I'm not married."

The cold, hard words were like nails being driven into Shontelle's heart. Had she made a mistake? A flood of hot turmoil hit her. Fortunately she'd reached the window. She swiftly turned her back on him, hiding her wretched confusion, pretending to be captivated by the spectacular view.

Surely to God he was lying! He'd been betrothed to another woman—the Gallardo heiress—before and during their affair two years ago. He'd lied then, by omission. He'd left Shontelle blindly believing she was the only woman who counted in his life when there were two others who had a longer, deeper claim on him.

How could anyone not count Elvira Rosa Martinez?

More to the point, it had been totally unconscionable of Luis to remain silent about the young woman designated as his wife; the sweet, convent-raised, beautifully mannered Claudia Gallardo.

His silence had spelled out where Shontelle stood in his life—a handy bit of foreign fluff on the side, out of his mainstream, suitable only for fun and relaxation. But then he hadn't made any promises, she savagely reminded herself.

"I assume you're not married, either, since you're travelling with your brother," he drawled, each word sounding closer.

He was coming after her.

"I'm here on business, Luis," she said tersely, wishing she hadn't raised anything personal. He couldn't be believed anyway. He'd undoubtedly say—or not say—whatever suited his purpose.

"Do you have a lover tucked away at home, waiting to serve your inclinations?" His voice had the stinging flick of a whip.

"I'm all out of lovers at the moment," she answered flippantly, disdaining even a glance at him.

"Which is why you came on this trip, mmh?"

The silky taunt hit her on the raw. The urge to swing around and let him have the sting of her tongue almost blew her mind off her purpose here. She gritted her teeth, folded her arms to hold wayward impulses in, and stared fixedly at the myriad of lights beyond the window.

"It looks like a fairyland outside, doesn't it?" she remarked as lightly as she could.

It was true. La Paz was the highest capital in the

world and it appeared to be built in a moon crater.
From where she was viewing it from the low down-
town area, the lights of the city rose in a great circular
curve, going up so high they seemed to be hanging
in the sky. Incredible there were actually people living behind them.

"You need a magician to get you out of it," Luis
mocked, standing right behind her now.

"We need a bus," she said quickly, fighting her
intense awareness of his nearness.

"The curfew doesn't lift until six in the morning."

Her heart skittered. What was he implying? They
had all night to negotiate?

"I don't like your hair constricted in a plait," was
his next comment, confusing Shontelle further.

Her spine crawled at his touch as he lifted the rope
of hair away from her back. She knew what he was
going to do but her mind couldn't accept it. He
couldn't still love her hair. He couldn't still *want* her!

Or maybe he didn't.

Maybe he was playing some cruel cat-and-mouse
game.

She wanted to look at his face but she was frightened to. What if he was waiting to feed off her feelings? Pride insisted she deny him the satisfaction of
knowing she was rattled. Could he hear the mad
thumping of her heart? Stay calm, stay calm, stay
calm, she recited feverishly.

He'd worked off the rubber band and was separat-
ing the twisted swathes, seeming to take sensual plea-

sure in the feel of her hair. Impossible to ignore it. Impossible to stay calm.

"What do you want from me, Luis?" she blurted out.

"What I had before."

Her mind fragmented under the force of her own desire to have him again, and his apparent desire to recall and repeat the passion they'd shared. Some tattered shreds of reason shrieked that he was only playing with her, using his power to make her succumb to him, but she had to know, had to see.

As she jerked around to face him, her arms flew out of their protective fold and lifted into an instinctive plea for truth. "What do you mean?" she cried.

He still held a skein of her hair and he wound it around his hand as his eyes blazed their dark purpose into hers. "I mean to seize the day, Shontelle. Or to put it more graphically...the night. You want a bus. I want one more taste of you."

Shock waves slammed through her.

One more taste...

Only *one...*

Payment for the bus.

"Not such a difficult deal, is it?" he taunted. "Just a matter of giving me what you gave of yourself two years ago...in your desire to get what you wanted of me."

"I didn't get what I wanted then," she protested, her voice thin and shaky under the appalling weight of devastated hopes.

A savage fury flared into his eyes. "Was I not all you wanted of a Latin lover?" His mouth curled with cruel intent. "Well, let me try not to disappoint you tonight. We have many hours ahead of us. I promise you a feast of hot-blooded sensuality."

Hot and hard and ruthless.

The awful part was, Shontelle could not stop her body from pulsing with excitement at what he offered. Only with him had she ever known intense physical ecstasy. She hadn't even felt a twinge of attraction towards anyone else in the past two years. Just the thought of touching Luis again, feeling him…quivers of anticipation shot through her.

But he was treating her like a whore, laying it out that she could only get the bus in return for sex.

Sex…not remotely connected to love. Not even the slightest semblance of love. It was wrong, wrong, wrong! Her heart twisted in torment as he twisted her hair more firmly around his hand and tugged her closer to him. Then his other hand slid over her breasts, his palm rotating caressingly, his eyes glittering their triumphant knowledge of what had pleasured her in the past, and to prove him right, her nipples instantly stiffened into begging prominence.

"Stop it!" she hissed, hating his power to arouse her even as she revelled in the sharp sensation that stimulated a host of nerves, arcing from her breasts to the innermost core of her sexuality.

One black eyebrow arched mockingly. "You no longer like this?"

He was the devil incarnate, tempting her. The truth was, she didn't want him to stop. She didn't want him to ever stop. But he would. This was only to be one more taste. Unless...

Something deeply primitive stirred in Shontelle.

He wasn't married, so he said.

And he still wanted her.

He also wanted a payback for his wounded pride.

Well, so did she. So did she!

"I don't normally go for one night stands," she said.

"But these are special circumstances," he returned silkily.

"Just let me understand you clearly, Luis..."

With her heart thumping to a wild beat, Shontelle flicked open the shirt button over his chest curls and slid her hand inside, seeking and deliberately tweaking one of his nipples. His sharply indrawn breath was music to her ears. She had power over him, too. It wasn't a one-way street.

Her eyes flirted challengingly with his as she spoke through the provocative, physical teasing. "...If I stay with you the night and let you have your..." She lowered her gaze to his mouth, regarding it assessingly. "...taste of me..." She let the words linger for a moment, then flicked her gaze up, raising her eyebrows in pointed questioning. "...I get the bus? Is that the deal?"

"Yes," he hissed at her.

"Then make your calls now, Luis. Let me hear you

arrange the delivery of an appropriate bus to The Europa Hotel as soon as the curfew is lifted tomorrow. When you've done that, I'll call Alan to assure him everything's all right and I'll be staying with you until morning.''

His jawline tightened. His eyes narrowed. He didn't like her calling the shots, but he'd dealt her the cards, made the rules of the game, and Shontelle figured he couldn't fault her over playing them. A sense of triumph poured a burst of adrenalin through her veins. No one was a victim unless they allowed themselves to be.

She pursed her lips into a considering little smile. ''A feast of hot-blooded sensuality sounds good. I do hope you're up to it, Luis.''

The moment the words were out, she felt a swell of danger—a dark and fierce emanation from him swirling around her, sending shivers down her spine. He smiled right back at her as he released her hair— a smile that promised himself a deep well of satisfaction. He plucked her hand from inside his shirt and drew it slowly down, palm against him, fingers splayed.

''Feel for yourself how *up* to it I am, Shontelle,'' he drawled, his other hand gliding up her throat to cup her chin.

He was fully erect, his arousal straining against the barrier of clothes. He guided her into stroking him as he tilted her head and bent his own. ''Just to make sure I do want the taste,'' he murmured, then covered her mouth with his, not giving her any chance of reply.

Shontelle didn't even think of trying to deny him. The urge to taste him, too, was far too strong for any denial. And his mouth was soft, sweetly seductive, at first, his tongue merely flicking over the soft inner tissues of her lips, sensitising them with delicious tingles.

She responded, wanting to know if the passion they had once shared could be triggered again, beyond pride, beyond all the differences between them. Her free arm instinctively curled around his neck to hold him to her and the kiss deepened, pursuing a more erotic, more exciting intimacy.

Her body started clenching with a need it had all but forgotten. She grasped the hard proof of his desire, fingers digging around it, revelling in the feel of him. She was so caught up in her own strong responses, it came as a shock when he abruptly ended their kiss, removed her hand from him and broke out of her embrace.

"You must be hungry for a man, Shontelle," he mocked, lifting the fingers that had been squeezing him to his mouth. He lightly nipped them. "Definitely an appetising taste. Please excuse me while I execute my half of the deal. I look forward to the rest of the night."

He walked away from her, seemingly completely in control of himself. Shontelle was left feeling shattered, her legs trembling, drained of strength, her stomach churning so much she wanted to be sick, her heart aching, her mind zigzagging helplessly through a maze of fierce contradictions.

She loved him…and hated him.

She craved more of him…yet wanted to cut out his callous heart.

Was it to be a night of intense life…or a night of heart-killing desolation?

She didn't know…couldn't decide…couldn't tear herself away from whatever might pass between them.

He picked up a telephone, pressed a sequence of numbers, spoke with the arrogant authority of his name, his position, the power that came automatically with great wealth…Luis Angel Martinez…the only man who'd ever moved her like this…and maybe the only man who ever would.

Was there anything to win by staying?

The bus, her mind answered.

But the bus had no relevance to the question.

She wanted…needed…to win something for herself. So she had to stay and see this night through, even if she lost everything.

One night…one night…unless she could turn it into something more.

CHAPTER FOUR

LUIS was rock-hard and in pain but the shattered look he'd left on Shontelle's face was worth every second of the discomfort. No way was she going to turn the tables on him! He hoped the witch was burning with frustration.

He deliberately kept his back turned to her while he talked on the phone to Ramon Flores who could organize any form of road transport in La Paz. It was local courtesy to speak Quechua, the old Inca language, and Luis did so with perverse pleasure, knowing Shontelle would not be able to follow it. Her grasp of Spanish was good, but she only had a sketchy knowledge of the native dialects.

Let her stew in uncertainty, he thought. She was too damned sure of her power to get what she wanted. Before this night was out she'd learn who was master of the situation, and he'd kiss her goodbye with the same brutal finality she'd shown him two years ago.

"The bus is not a problem, Luis," Ramon said predictably. "But..."

The pause sharpened Luis' attention. "But what?"

"It would be useless to ask any of my local drivers to deliver it. They would be stopped and arrested before the bus got to The Europa. The military edict is no gathering of crowds. They consider three people

31

together a crowd. A local man taking out a bus…it would not be allowed. Too suspicious."

Luis frowned. He hadn't thought of that. Yet if he didn't deliver…no, he had to. He refused to look weak and ineffectual in front of Shontelle Wright. There had to be a way.

"Your Australian friend…he might get through, being a foreigner," Ramon suggested. "Since he is prepared to risk his tour group in trying to get out of La Paz, tell him to come to the depot and take the bus himself. It will be fully fuelled, ready to go."

It made sense, but it wasn't the deal he'd agreed to with Shontelle. Her words, not his, he reasoned. He didn't have to toe *her* line. The essence of the deal was the same. The bus would be available for Alan to take. That was all his erstwhile friend had requested.

"Someone will be at the depot to hand over the bus?" he asked.

"Curfew lifts at six. I'll have a man at the gates at six-thirty."

"Thank you, Ramon."

"Your friend is a fool, Luis."

"His choice."

"It's our bus. This could bring trouble kicking back to us."

"I'll wear it. You are simply following my orders, Ramon."

"As you wish."

Luis slowly lowered the receiver, his mind engaged in hard reappraisal. This whole enterprise was stupid, inviting trouble. Alan's tour group was safe at their hotel. What was another week or two out of their lives? Better locked away in luxury than dead. It was just as stupid for him to get involved, putting the Martinez reputation for finely balanced political sense on the line.

For what?

A woman who had used him...a woman worth nothing!

Madness to have been tempted into wreaking some sweet vengeance. It was beneath him. He should dismiss her from his suite right now, send her off with a bitter sense of failure. That was vengeance enough.

He turned to do it.

She stood framed by the blackness of the night beyond the window, the twinkling stars of light from the city surrounding her, lending her an air of etherial mystery. Her long hair gleamed like a stream of moonlight and her golden skin glowed, the perfect foil for eyes that shone like emeralds. Her full lips were slightly apart, as he'd left them, waiting it seemed for another kiss, insidiously beckoning him.

He forced his gaze down the long graceful line of her neck to the blood-red T-shirt. She had no heart, he told himself. No heart. But the lush softness of her breasts moved as though to the beat of one, a beat that tugged on him with inexorable and tormenting strength.

How was it possible, he wondered, to feel such desire for a woman...yet hate her with equal ferocity?

"Is the bus assured for tomorrow morning?" she asked, her voice strained.

The conviction swept into Luis' mind. This was no

fun for her. Which was only right and just. She'd had her *fun* last time. It was his turn tonight. He could send her away right now, defeated, but what satisfaction was there in that? He wanted—needed—the same physical satisfaction she had taken from him, over and over again.

"Yes," he said. "You'll get the bus."

Which put their deal on the line.

Luis watched her take that in, and all it implied. Her gaze dropped from the hard challenge in his. Her hands interlocked in front of her waist, as though testing how much strength she had, fingers flexing…and he craved their touch on him again. Her breasts and shoulders lifted slightly as she drew in a deep breath. He found himself holding his own breath, waiting for her decision, willing her to concede to him, his whole body focusing energy on her, determined on drawing her into the ring with him.

She spoke, still with her eyes downcast. "If you have a wife, Luis, this is a rotten game you're playing and I won't be a party to it."

Luis clenched his teeth. It was because of her he didn't have a wife, but he'd rot in hell before she dragged that admission from him.

"If I had a wife, you would have had no access to me, Shontelle," he stated bitingly.

Her lashes slowly lifted, her eyes meeting his with an oddly poignant expression of irony. He caught a sense of fatalism, yet there was no resignation to defeat in it, more a feeling of being ready to ride whatever outcome ensued from the situation. It disturbed him. It wasn't what he expected from her. Not what he wanted, either.

"What time should I tell Alan the bus will be at our hotel?" she asked. "He'll want to have the tour group ready to go."

The hotel! It was on the tip of his tongue to state that Alan would have to collect the bus from the depot. A surge of pride stopped him. If he didn't win his ground with this woman, he would always feel whipped by her. Which was totally intolerable. No way would he give Shontelle Wright any cause to scorn him again.

It might be sheer madness to risk his own skin to balance the scales, madness to risk blotting the Martinez reputation for steering clear of trouble, but he would get the damned bus himself rather than give Shontelle a loophole out of this deal. She had to be his for this one night. Somehow it was a need that drove to the very core of his manhood.

"Seven o'clock," he answered tersely. "Given that it's not stopped by the military. That I cannot control."

A sigh whispered from her lips. She nodded acceptance. "Fair enough! I'll ring Alan now."

Done!

Yet Luis' triumph had a bittersweet taste. She had wrung more from him than she was worth. But she would pay, he promised himself. He would strip her of every bit of power she had over him before dawn came. Then he would be free of her. Finally free of her.

CHAPTER FIVE

SHONTELLE tried desperately to focus her mind on how to tell Alan she was spending the night with the man who'd stolen her heart two years ago and hadn't valued it...a man who'd used her for pleasure...and when she'd taken the pleasure away, had vindictively taken out his displeasure on her brother. There was simply no way Alan was going to understand.

One more night...

With any luck she should at least win something from this encounter. It would either set her free of Luis Angel Martinez...or...give her hope of something more from him, more than she had believed possible.

He *wanted* her...perhaps as badly as she wanted him. It was what she was gambling on. Plus the fact he hadn't married. The Gallardo heiress hadn't got him. And maybe—just maybe—Elvira Rosa Martinez didn't know her son as well as she thought she did.

''The telephone is free for you to use,'' Luis dryly reminded her, gesturing to it with a casual grace that belied any tension on his part over her decision to stay.

He looked so arrogantly sure of himself.

But he did want her.

Shontelle pushed her legs into action and a wry smile onto her mouth. "This is not going to be an easy call."

He returned a derisive look. "Did you think it was easy, looking like a fool for ordering a bus out in this volatile climate?"

He had a point.

Both of them fools.

For some reason, that thought boosted Shontelle's morale.

Luis did not move away from the telephone to let her speak privately to Alan. He propped himself against the edge of the writing desk, apparently intent on hearing every word. She had no choice but to stand next to him, which heightened her awareness of the strong force field coming from his dominating maleness.

She turned her back on him once the call was put through. She didn't want him witnessing her awkwardness in explaining her decision to Alan. It was bad enough knowing he was listening without him watching her every nuance of expression.

"Where are you calling from?" Alan demanded, the moment she announced herself.

"I'm still with Luis in his suite. He's got you the bus, Alan."

"What did he want for it?"

"It's no problem. You can tell everyone to be in the hotel foyer, ready to leave at seven o'clock, all going well."

"All going well?" Suspicion sharpened his voice. "What's Luis up to, Shontelle?"

"Alan, he's ordered the bus. He can't guarantee the military won't stop it before it reaches the hotel."

She heard him expel a long breath. She also heard Luis straighten away from the desk, moving to stand behind her.

"Right! That's it then," Alan decided. "I take it you've finished talking and you're ready to leave. Give me five minutes and I'll be at the side door into the Plaza to bring you back here."

Hands slid around her waist, distracting her. Luis was standing close behind her, very close, but not touching except for his hands. Her buttocks clenched in sheer nervousness. Her heart leapt into her throat when he started unbuckling her belt.

"Shontelle?"

She dragged her attention back to Alan, belatedly recalling he'd been offering the protection of his escort back to the hotel.

"Uh...no. No, we haven't finished here," she rushed out.

"Just starting," Luis murmured, darkly purred words that set her pulse pounding. The buckle undone, he unbuttoned the waistband and drew down her zipper.

Shontelle held her breath. Her mind blanked out on all active thought, waiting, poised on the edge of an explosion of sensation should he move his hand inside her clothes and...

"What's going on there?" Alan demanded, his voice getting edgier.

She gulped, forced herself to think. An answer was needed. Fast. "I'm going to spend the night with Luis, Alan," she gabbled, almost yelping as her trousers and underpants were pulled down to her thighs.

"What?" Alan squawked.

Her brother's shock was nothing to Shontelle's at being so summarily stripped. Exposed. Vulnerable to anything Luis might choose to do with her. This was going too far, too fast. The urge to drop the telephone and yank up her clothes was muddled by Alan's yelling at her.

"I'm coming to get you right now."

"No!" She jerked around to face Luis, wanting to stop his actions, too. "No!" she repeated for him.

Wild, reckless and wicked intent blazed at her. He ignored her protest, picked her up, sat her bare bottom on the desk, lifted one of her legs, propped her foot against his thigh and proceeded to undo her bootlace. Shontelle lost track of what she should be doing. Luis was undressing her with ruthless efficiency. His powerfully muscled thigh was bent towards her, reminding her of how magnificently perfect his physique was. But shouldn't she stop this...this taking? If she moved her foot up...

"Shontelle..." Alan bellowed in her ear. "...If this is the bargain he's struck with you..."

"Alan, I've done your business," she cut in, frantic to be free of the argument. "This is mine and Luis' business and it's completely personal. Personal! Got that?'' she snapped.

Her shoe and sock were off. Luis was lifting her other leg.

''Are you off your brain? Luis will chew you up and spit you out again,'' Alan thundered at her.

Once both her feet were free, he would remove her clothes and…there was no time for appeasing Alan. Couldn't be done anyway. Just watching Luis' deft, ruthless movements, she was torn between excitement and fear, yet swamping both feelings was a compelling need to know all she wanted to know.

''Let him do it then!'' she cried recklessly.

''Is he holding the deal with the bus over you?'' Anxious now…

Better for her to sound sane…though her trousers and underpants were being tugged down her calves, over her ankles. She struggled for breath, struggled for some final words.

''Do me a favour, Alan, and pack my bags so they're ready to go. I'll come back when the curfew lifts in the morning.''

Luis stepped in between her legs, his eyes glittering at her, exultant, revelling in seizing the moment, the night, her, everything…making it his.

''Shontelle, for God's sake! Will you…''

Luis seized the telephone. ''Stay out of this, Alan!'' he commanded. ''Your sister and I have much to work through and it's very, very personal.''

There was no argument with Luis. He simply didn't

allow it, cutting the connection by slamming the receiver down. Without so much as a pause, he grabbed the bottom of her T-shirt and hauled it off her. Shontelle's arms were still coming down as his hands whipped around her back to unclip her bra. No fumbling. Snap, and her last piece of clothing dangled loose and was swiftly consigned to the pile on the floor.

She was completely naked, dazed by the speed of its happening and the total lack of any sensuality accompanying the stripping of clothes. She stared at Luis' face and saw a mask of hard pride...dark, dark Angel.

He gave her no time to think, speak, question. He gripped her rib cage, hoisted her off the desk and carrying her virtually at arm's length, he strode through the suite to the bedroom. Impossible for Shontelle to find purchase for her arms or legs. They flapped uselessly. She was so stunned at being held like some distasteful object, any sense of coordination was utterly lost. He tossed her on the bed and she bounced into an abandoned sprawl.

''That's where I want you,'' he said, his voice harsh with the effort expended. He lifted his shoulders back, holding an imperious, superior stance by the bed. ''Where you should be...'' he went on with savagely mocking emphasis, ''...on the playing ground you use so well.''

Scathing words, scathing eyes as they travelled slowly over her. They spurred Shontelle into a clear recognition of his fierce drive to pay her back for having regarded him as no more than a good lay. Even lower than that…a transient lay who'd worn out his novelty value. The Latin lover tag had remained a burr under his skin.

But deeper than that…was *she* still under his skin?

He was holding control, determined on keeping the upper hand, but how much feeling for her lay behind his armoured pride? If she could break through…

She moved sinuously, provocatively, arranging herself more comfortably on the bed, looping her hair over one shoulder so it streamed across her breasts. "You were quite a masterful player yourself, Luis," she said with a reminiscent smile, idly moving a tress of hair back and forth over one of her nipples. "A pity you seem to have lost your touch." She deliberately ran her gaze over his body as she added, "Brute strength is rather a sad step down."

A mirthless laugh scraped from his throat. "In your search for variety, I'm sure a bit of rough has featured somewhere." His eyes glittered challengingly at her as he stripped off his shirt. "I thought it might give you a kick since you grew bored with my kind of lovemaking."

"I was never bored with you," she said truthfully. "I thought what we shared was very special."

A flash of derision. "So you left before it got spoiled."

It was spoiled *before she left*. "The writing was on the wall, Luis," she said quietly, remembering how naive she'd been not to even see it until it was pointed out to her. "I got out before it fell on top of me."

"What writing?" he jeered, bending to remove his shoes and socks, his body language clearly contemptuous of any excuse she might offer.

"Your real life in Buenos Aires," Shontelle said, testing for some flash of guilt from him for what he'd kept hidden.

There was no sharp glance at her. He finished taking off his footwear and when he straightened up, his dark eyes gloated over her with unmistakably sexual intent...such burning intent Shontelle squirmed inside.

"I see," he drawled. "Our romantic idyll on the Amazon was over. I had work to do in Buenos Aires so you did not get my full attention there. Rest assured you have it tonight, Shontelle."

He proceeded to unfasten his trousers.

"Why?" she shot at him, frustrated at being relegated to a sexual object. Though that might be all he'd ever thought of her. The urge to sting him as she was stung slid straight off her tongue. "Your other women not delivering any spice, Luis? You need a taste of me to supplement your diet?"

It stung him all right. His mouth thinned for a moment and there was a flare of anger in his eyes, giving her a glimpse of a banked inner rage that promised no quarter given tonight.

"You think you're special, Shontelle?" He left the lilt of mockery hanging while he finished undressing.

Then stark naked, powerfully naked, aggressively naked, he gave her a smile that curled with vengeful satisfaction. "Well, yes you are," he drawled. "A rich, erotic indulgence...so special I think I should make a banquet of you."

And spit me out in the morning.

Shontelle's stomach was suddenly a hollow pit. All the cards looked black in this game—clubs and spades—no hearts, no diamonds. Even so, she could not give up all hope. Not yet.

"Taking a risk, aren't you?" she slung back at him. "People get addicted to rich, erotic indulgences."

He laughed, and despite its being dark amusement, his face was suddenly transformed into the lighter, more lovable Luis she had known, and Shontelle's heart tripped over itself. Her body wantonly buzzed with anticipation as he prowled onto the bed, looming over her, sweeping her hair away from her breasts, raking it into a fan around her head, his eyes simmering with lustful heat.

"A substance has to be readily available for one to become addicted," he murmured, sipping seductively at her lips. "I'll just take all I can get of it tonight."

Readily available...the phrase echoed in Shontelle's ears as Luis fully engaged her mouth with his in a long, devouring kiss, stirring her hunger for him, a hunger that had been starved for two miserable, empty years. If she'd stayed, maybe he would have defied his heritage to keep her. Foolish pride... walking out on him without confronting him with what she'd been told, what he'd withheld. An open choice would have been better, cleaner.

Maybe with this second chance…

She raked her fingers through his hair, revelling in the feel of it, a huge surge of possessiveness welling through her. This man was *hers,* had to be. There was no other like him. And he had to feel the same about her. It had to be mutual, this passionate craving.

Then suddenly her hands were snatched away, slammed onto the bed and pinned above her head as he levered himself up. "It's *my* night, Shontelle."

She looked into eyes seething with dark turbulence.

"And the playing will be all mine."

He bent and licked her lips as though collecting the lingering evidence of her response to his kiss, then trailed his mouth slowly down to the pulse at the base of her throat, pausing there to apply a heated pressure that kicked her heart into wilder pumping.

Satisfied, he moved lower to the taut mounds of her breasts, tilted up by the lifted position of her arms. He subjected them to exquisite torment—teasing tongue-lashing, voluptuous suction, sharp little nips— orchestrating such a varied rush of sensations, Shontelle had no mind to protest the ruling he'd made. She was awash with rippling excitement, too enthralled with experiencing Luis again to care how or why he was feasting on her…as long as he kept doing it.

Even when he took one imprisoning hand from hers, she didn't try to touch him. He was touching...tantalising, circular caresses over and around her stomach, dipping lower, lower, fingers sliding through the silky mound of hair, stroking, parting, slowly seeking the sensitive moist place that yearned for his touch.

And he was so good at it...softly sensual, as though he was acutely attuned to how much arousal her nerve-ends could take at a time, and he matched the rhythm of his stroking to the tug of his mouth on her breasts, building a momentum that held Shontelle utterly enthralled, focused so intensely on what he was making her feel, there was no room for anything else, no time.

All vestige of control over herself slipped away under the sweet onslaught of sensation. Muscles quivered. The ache of need soared into an urgent scream for the ultimate path to be taken. She was more than ready for him. The inner convulsions were starting and he wasn't there yet. Not the part of him she wanted most, the intimate connection that would take her with him on the final climb to ecstasy.

"Luis...please..." The cry burst from her throat, shamelessly begging.

He reacted fast, so fast she didn't even begin to comprehend what he intended to happen. He flipped her body face down, pushed her legs apart with his knees, curled one arm around her stomach and hauled her backwards, her thighs sliding past his as he rocked back on his ankles, her bottom pressing up against his stomach. She felt him position himself for entry, felt her own flesh quiver in eagerness for the promise of him, a totally out-of-control response. The penetration came hard and fast and incredibly deep as he pushed her down on him, taking an angle he'd never taken before, making her feel the passage of every inch of him rushing further and further inside her. Then he arced her body back with his to make her feel it even more intensely.

He rocked her with him—forward, back, up, down—Shontelle was both shocked and shaken by the sheer animal wildness of this coupling, yet acutely aware of sensations she'd never felt before, bombarded by a physicality she hadn't even imagined, and hopelessly distracted by the sheer strength of him both enveloping and invading her.

Every time he drew back he left one strongly controlling arm around her waist, hand splayed across her stomach, pressing in, keeping her hugged tightly to him as he moved almost to the point of losing intimate contact. Then came the hard thrust forward again, the weird, sweet sense of shattering inside her as he drove himself back to the inner centre, and the hand on her stomach held the fullness of him there as though emphasising a claim of absolute possession, relishing it, filling her with the sense of him filtrating every cell of her body.

He repeated the action—Shontelle had no idea how many times. Occasionally when he paused at the innermost point, he slid his other hand over her breasts, cupping them, squeezing them, fanning her nipples, rubbing her hair over them, or he kissed the nape of her neck, making her shiver from the sheer intensity of his *tasting,* while deep within her a storm of ecstatic waves flowed and ebbed, wild, turbulent, impossible to stop.

She didn't care that he controlled everything. The incredible chaos he wreaked on her was beyond anything she'd ever known. It didn't matter when he carried her forward to kneel underneath him, taking the freedom to drive to his own climax in a fiercely pummelling rhythm.

She was so soft and mushy inside, she welcomed the fast stirring of more sensation, the feeling of violent desire being answered by what he found in her, the surging power of it, coming and coming and coming until he spilled the essence of his strength into her and she exulted in receiving it because there was no taking this back. He was hers as much as she was his.

He scooped her to him spoon-fashion as he dropped onto the bed to rest. There was no parting, no letting go. Her head was tucked under his chin, his arms around her. It didn't occur to her that he had used her as his plaything. Her mind was completely fuzzed with the sense of being one with him.

Luis Angel…dark, light…it didn't matter. He was her man. And as he began stroking her again, arousing both of them to a pitch of needful excitement, she thought only that he wanted more of her.

But…he stopped her from making love to him. He

blocked every initiative she started to take. He controlled the moves. He chose how, when and where he tasted her. And Shontelle gradually lost all sense of being one with him. The realisation came like cold claws creeping around her heart, squeezing out the hope she'd nursed.

This was, indeed, his feast. It wasn't mutual. He hadn't meant it to be mutual. She was the food and he was taking it as he liked, sampling whatever appealed to his fancy, sating himself with every aspect of her sexuality. He didn't care what she was feeling, except in so far as it increased his pleasure, his satisfaction, his sense of being master of the situation, master of *her*.

The answer she'd sought was staring her in the face.

There was no future for her with Luis Angel Martinez.

There was nothing for her here.

Nothing.

With that absolute conviction, Shontelle found the strength to fight free of him, jabbing her elbows into his body, kicking and shoving herself out of contact, scrambling off the bed. She heard him curse in Spanish but she didn't stop. Choosing the bathroom as the safest refuge, she sped into it and locked the door behind her.

She was a tremulous mess, a hopeless tremulous mess. Nevertheless, there was one thing she could and would hold firm—the fierce resolution to deny Luis Angel Martinez any further chance of using her as he willed. Regardless of anything he said or did, she would not return to *his* playing ground.

CHAPTER SIX

SHONTELLE'S fast and frantic evasion of him took Luis completely by surprise—a decidedly unwelcome and frustrating one. It came without any apparent reason—compliance suddenly exploding into rejection. However, the slamming of the bathroom door was so jarring, it propelled him into a swift review of what he'd been doing.

She hadn't cried out, hadn't complained or protested. He couldn't have hurt her physically. Every step of the way her body had responded positively, not once baulking at submitting to his pursuit of every desire he'd harboured when thinking of her. No...he shook off the niggle of concern...he had not hurt her.

So why had she cut and run?

He'd certainly stopped her from weaving her seductive power over him. No way would he allow her to treat him as her toy-boy again. He'd made that clear from the start. Though she probably hadn't believed him immune to her charms. More than likely that had finally bit in—no leeway given for Shontelle to get her hooks into him.

He shrugged, dismissing the annoyance of having his game-plan thwarted. Let her sulk in the bathroom. Let her rage. If she thought she was making some stand against his domination of proceedings, she'd soon find out it was impossible to wring any concession from him. Besides, he'd already done what he'd set out to do, and enjoyed every second of it, too. He wasn't about to beg for more.

He smiled with grim satisfaction as he swung his legs off the bed.

She'd begged.

And he'd given it to her.

Right to the hilt.

He hoped she'd remember that to her dying day. Luis Martinez was not a man to trifle with.

The clock on the bedside table read 11:47. Not even midnight yet. So much for Shontelle's agreeing to give him the night. Another cheat from her. All promise...no staying power. Typical.

He collected the hotel's complimentary bathrobe from the cupboard, put it on, wrapped it around his nakedness to ward off the night chill, and headed for the sitting room and the minibar.

As he passed the bathroom he heard the shower running. Trying to wash him off, he thought sardonically. If there was any justice in the world, she'd be no more successful than he'd been in washing her off the past two years.

The lights were still on in the sitting room. Shontelle's clothes were on the floor. Luis viewed the litter of female garments with a sense of black humour as he moved past them to pour himself a drink. Shontelle wasn't going anywhere without dressing herself first. Sooner or later, she'd come out of the bathroom and collect her clothing. That should be an interesting moment.

He heaped more sugar than usual over the slices of lime for his drink. Vengeance was supposed to be sweet, but it wasn't, Luis decided. It reinforced the bitter taste of knowing what was really wanted was beyond reach. Hopelessly beyond reach.

He took his drink over to the picture window and stared out at the lights of La Paz—quite stunningly beautiful, a fairyland, as Shontelle put it. Just like her, Luis thought savagely, a deceptive facade, offering magic, hiding the power to blow him apart.

Tomorrow morning he'd have to face the streets down there, walk them unprotected in order to get to the bus depot. It would be more dangerous once he was behind the wheel of the bus. A stupid deal…all for the sake of one more experience of Shontelle, with him ending up the winner.

Utterly stupid…when there was nothing to win. She'd made that clear last time. No love in her heart for him. Just sex. Sex he'd once believed was entwined with something much deeper…so deep it was still playing hell with him. What joy now in his vengeful drive to expunge that tormenting residue of feeling? He shook his head in self-derision. A brief savage pleasure…leaving him empty.

He sipped his drink and decided he didn't care if he died on the streets of La Paz tomorrow.

He just didn't care.

CHAPTER SEVEN

SHONTELLE switched off the bathroom light, turned the knob as quietly as she could and slowly eased the door open, listening acutely for any sound coming from the rest of Luis' suite. She held her breath. Her heartbeat seemed to be thumping in her ears but she couldn't hear any other movement going on.

Had Luis given up on her and gone to sleep?

Shontelle vehemently prayed it was so. She'd been in the bathroom over an hour, trying to get herself back together, vigorously cleaning off every possible vestige of Luis' tasting, even washing and blow-drying her long hair in a compulsive need to rid it of any touch of him. She would replait it, as well, once she found the rubber band Luis had taken off.

Clutching the top edge of the bath towel she'd fastened around her nakedness, she plucked up a brave front, slid out into the short passageway that linked the bedroom to the sitting room, and headed swiftly into the latter. The lights had been left on. She had no trouble spotting her clothes.

As distasteful as she found having to dress in the same things Luis had stripped off her, there was no other choice in these circumstances. She wanted a barrier established fast, one Luis couldn't fail to recognise, and she'd fight him tooth and nail if he tried to tear it away.

Pants, trousers, bra, T-shirt…she hastily pulled them on, discarding the towel as she donned more protective gear. Rather than waste a second in fully covering herself, she sat on the floor to put on her socks and shoes. Then feeling more in control and less at risk, she climbed to her feet and turned to assess the supposedly comfortable seating near the window, intending to spend the rest of the night there.

Her swinging gaze didn't get that far.

It halted, very abruptly, at the passageway to the bedroom.

Shock ripped through her, throwing her into chaos again; every nerve-end twitching with agitation, every muscle tensing, every logical thought in her head jamming into confusion. Her eyes stayed glued to the man dominating the space she had desperately wanted to stay empty, the man whose presence could only mean more trauma for her, the man who'd systematically destroyed what had once been good between them.

He hadn't just arrived. Shontelle knew instantly he'd been watching her, standing there watching her as she'd scrambled to get into her clothes…another humiliation added to the humiliations he'd heaped on her. It was some relief that he was no longer naked, though the white bathrobe—so pure and clean-looking—formed an ironic contrast to the dark, satanically beautiful face of Luis Angel Martinez. There was no relief, however, to her fear of what was brooding behind it.

There was a less controlled air about him now, hair mussed, wavy strands dipping over his forehead, curling around his ears. The brilliant dark eyes no longer burned with purpose. They were shadowed by his thick lashes but seemed to emit a sardonic gleam— mocking her, mocking himself, mocking the world and everything in it.

"I take it you don't intend to rejoin me in my bed," he drawled.

"You've had your pound of flesh, Luis," she flashed at him, too worked up to temper her words.

He shrugged. "I've lost my taste for it anyway."

She burned under the contempt implicit in his words, contempt for what she had tried to give him, however misled she had been. "Good!" she snapped. "I've lost any taste for you, too."

He waved carelessly towards the door that led out of the suite. "Do feel free to leave anytime you like."

Her fury at his treatment of her sliced straight into bitter scorn. "Oh, sure! So you can welch on the deal."

"Your staying here any longer is now quite irrelevant," he said in a bored tone. "If you're afraid to brave the streets, by all means call your brother. I assume he's prepared to escort you back to your hotel."

"No!" she retorted vehemently, hating him with the same force as she had once loved him. "I'll stay until curfew lifts in the morning, as I agreed. Having been used by you as no better than a whore, I will not give you any loophole to weazel out of paying what you promised.''

She'd hold him to the damned bus if it killed her. He wasn't going to get away with taking her as he had for nothing.

The cold mask of pride resettled on his face. ''I gave you my word.''

''I'll see how well you keep it in the morning.'' Her eyes blistered any worth in his *given word*. ''Since you're finding no more pleasure in my company than I am in yours, I suggest you go back to your bed and I'll settle myself here.''

''Thank you,'' he mocked. ''Do sleep well with your choice of discomfort.''

He strolled off to the bedroom, leaving Shontelle feeling wretchedly deflated. Clearly he now saw her as a waste of his time, not even worth arguing with. For several moments she teetered on the edge of going after him, flaying him with her own contempt for his lies and double-dealing, but what was the point?

He didn't care.

That was the bottom line.

He simply didn't care.

Even if she stayed until the curfew was lifted, it was no guarantee he would follow through on his word, but at least she would have fulfilled her part. If she took nothing else away from this night, she would take her own integrity intact.

Nursing this shred of pride, Shontelle walked over to the window and searched the floor for the rubber band Luis had taken from her plait. Somehow it was important to restore her appearance to what it had been before she'd come here. She looked everywhere without success and finally concluded Luis had pocketed it. Which defeated her.

Defeat all round, she thought despondently, moving back to the writing desk. She picked up the telephone and made a request for a 5:45 wake-up call. It would mean Luis being woken, too, which she'd have to weather, since it served the purpose of letting him know she had stayed the full night.

Reassured of not oversleeping the mark, she proceeded to switch off the lights. The window provided a dim glow, enough to see her way by. She pulled two armchairs together, curled up on one and rested her legs on the other. Hoping fatigue would be her friend tonight, she closed her eyes and prayed for sleep.

But tears welled out of the devastation in her heart. Tears oozed through her lashes and trickled down her cheeks. Silent tears. Lonely tears. Tears that needed to be wept now because tomorrow she had to be strong again. It was a long time before sleep wiped them away and gave her some brief peace.

''Shontelle...''

The sharp call of her name brought her awake. Her

eyelids felt glued together but she dragged them open and looked up blearily.

Luis was standing by her chair, frowning at her.

Her brain was sluggish. Why was he waking her? Then her nose picked up the tangy scent of male cologne and she suddenly realised he was freshly showered, shaved, and fully dressed! Which had to mean she had somehow overslept and he was annoyed at finding she was still here.

She pushed the leg-rest armchair away and scrambled to her feet, crying out, "What time is it?" panicking at the thought of Alan waiting for her, worrying...

"Time enough," Luis answered brusquely. "It's not quite five-thirty. I've ordered breakfast. I thought you might like to refresh yourself before it arrives."

"Breakfast...for me?" she repeated dazedly.

"For both of us."

A knock on the door heralded its arrival and he turned away, moving quickly to let the waiter in. Shontelle stared at his back, flummoxed by this turn of events. He wore a navy shirt, navy trousers, navy Reeboks. What was he ready for this early in the morning?

The question nagged at her as she headed for the bathroom, needing to use its facilities to get herself ready for the day ahead. When she looked at her face in the mirror, she fiercely wished Luis had kept to himself in his bedroom. The whites of her eyes were red-rimmed and the skin around them was obviously puffy. Hating the thought he might have noticed this evidence of prolonged weeping, she did all she could to diminish it, splashing the area copiously with cold water.

Her hair was a flyaway mess but that didn't matter. She finger-combed it into reasonable tidiness. Having straightened up her crumpled clothes and composed herself to face Luis this one last time, she hurried out of the bathroom, anxious to know what his plans were.

Breakfast was laid out on the table in the sitting room. Luis was already seated and helping himself to the food he'd ordered. He glanced sharply at her face as she approached, his dark eyes uncomfortably penetrating.

"I've poured your coffee," he said matter-of-factly.

"Thank you." The reply was automatic, though she hated the reminder of how intimately acquainted they had once been and nothing would induce her to accept anything he offered at this point.

He gestured to the chair opposite his when she made no move to sit at the table. "Don't stand on ceremony, Shontelle. You might as well eat what's here."

"I'm not hungry." Which was true. "I put a wake-up call in for 5:45. I didn't expect you to be up so early."

"I'll be leaving the hotel as soon as curfew lifts," he answered offhandedly.

Alarm jangled through Shontelle's mind. Was Luis skipping out so he couldn't be called to account on the bus? "To go where?" she asked. "La Paz is shut down."

He shrugged. "Personal business."

She watched him crunch into a croissant and her stomach churned over his indifference to Alan's and her urgent concerns. "What if the bus doesn't come at seven o'clock? Where will you be?" she demanded testily.

He gave her a devil-may-care look. "Who knows?"

"That's not good enough, Luis," she shot at him, incensed by his blasé attitude.

His mouth tilted into an ironic curl. "It's as good as it gets, Shontelle. Take it or leave it."

No...she couldn't. She just couldn't. The pain and frustration she'd been holding in reached overload and streamed out over everything else, sweeping pride aside, demolishing any reasonable common sense, demanding an outlet. Her mouth opened and her voice shook with the force of feeling he'd brought her to.

"I never used you as you used me last night. I don't know why you think you have the right to play with me as it suits you, but I will not walk away from your lies and evasions this time."

That jolted his appetite. He stopped eating and glared at her.

Shontelle's throat felt scraped raw but the compulsion to throw down the gauntlet kept the words coming. "I'll follow you when you leave this hotel. I'll haunt you until the bus you promised turns up on The Europa doorstep. I'll…"

"What lies?" he demanded tersely.

"Don't you dare pretend you haven't lied!" His question was like a fire bomb going off in her brain. Old wounds ruptured and demanded to be aired. "Very convenient for you, wasn't it, to forget Claudia Gallardo while you were with me."

"I am not married to her," he bit out.

"*Betrothed* was the word your mother used. Your mother, whom you so carefully screened me from all the time I lived with you in Buenos Aires. Your mother, who explained your *real* life to me."

"When was this?" he snapped.

"The day before I left you. After you excluded me once again from your family life, Luis, evading the invitation your mother extended."

He erupted from his chair, dark menace emanating from him so strongly, Shontelle almost shrank from him. But she would not be intimidated. It was she who had the high moral ground, he who had to answer for his actions.

"You kept this from me," he accused.

"You kept it from me," she retaliated.

"You let my meddling, manipulative mother lay it waste. Without consulting me. You let Elvira have her way without so much as raising a question."

His seething fury rattled Shontelle.

"No heart!" he roared at her. "No faith! No trust! And for *you* I risk my life!"

She stared at him, mesmerised by the powerful surge of energy pouring from him, understanding nothing of what was causing it.

"Your life?" she echoed dazedly.

His chin jerked up. Pride emerged in a fierce blaze. Not cold pride. Not arrogant pride. Shontelle sensed this was his entire manhood on the line.

"Go back to your hotel," he commanded in a tone that brooked no opposition. "Wait with your brother. If I do not arrive with your bus, it will not be for the want of trying."

"You? You'll be driving the bus?"

He'd already turned his back on her, striding towards the door. Her disbelief was unanswered. He did not so much as pause.

"Luis!" she cried, suddenly torn by the feeling she would never see him again and there was too much left unanswered. Far too much.

He opened the door, stepped out, and was gone, the door closed firmly between them.

Shontelle struggled to get her shell-shocked wits together.

Nothing made sense to her anymore.

She didn't know what to believe.

If Luis turned up with the bus…what then?

Go back to your hotel. Wait with your brother.

That command made sense.

Besides, there was nothing else to do here.

Luis was gone.

CHAPTER EIGHT

ALAN was in the foyer of The Europa, obviously watching out for her while keeping an eye on the progress of checkouts at the desk. He was at Shontelle's side the moment she cleared the front door.

"Are you okay?" he asked, sharply scanning her face.

"I'm fine." She kept walking, making a beeline for the elevators, determined on not discussing anything personal with her brother. "Are my bags still in our suite?"

"Yes. I thought you'd want to change clothes."

"I do. I'll need the door key."

He handed it to her.

"Thanks. Won't be long."

"Shontelle…"

"Luis has gone to get the bus," she cut in, blocking what might have been an unwelcome inquiry.

"Luis has?" Stunned surprise.

"He said if it's not here by seven, it won't be for want of trying. Where is everyone?"

Alan was still shaking his head over Luis' personal involvement. "Those not paying their accounts at the desk are having breakfast in the dining room," he answered distractedly. "You'd better grab some, too, Shontelle. Long day ahead."

She pressed the up button on the elevator. Luck was on her side. The doors opened immediately. "Did you get the hotel to pack some food for us?" she tossed at Alan as she stepped into the compartment.

"Yes. Everything's organised. Shontelle..."

"Be down soon," she promised, activating the control panel.

The doors closed, shutting out Alan's frowning face.

Shontelle breathed a sigh of relief. She'd told him everything pertinent to the tour group situation. As for the rest...Luis might have some justification for thinking badly of her...if his mother had lied...and if Claudia Gallardo had conspired with Elvira Rosa Martinez to give a false impression. Where the truth actually lay was impossible for Shontelle to sort out.

Two facts stood out very starkly from all the grey areas. If she had told Luis of his mother's intervention two years ago, there would be no confusion about his feelings now. The blame for that was fairly and squarely on her shoulders. Nevertheless, even granting he had reason to think of her in the worst possible light, Luis should not have treated her as he had last night. That was unforgivable.

So there was no point in agonising over this encounter with him. Any future they might have had together was well and truly dead. It was time to lay the whole affair between them to rest. It was doubtful she'd ever forget her regrets, but she could accept he was gone from her life.

Though if he brought the bus himself...Shontelle felt her nerves tighten. He would only be here for a few minutes, she told herself, just long enough to hand the bus over to Alan. He'd walk away then. No trauma. It would only be a few minutes at most. *If* he came with the bus.

The elevator stopped and opened to her floor as she was frowning over this scenario. It wasn't until she was in her suite and digging into her bag that she attached Luis' claim about risking his life to the procuring of the bus. Yet was it what he'd meant? Was it so dangerous in the streets? Surely Alan wouldn't have decided on this course if the risk was truly grave.

She knew her brother expected to deal with some trouble on the way out of La Paz, but he was confident of steering them through it. Surely with the clout of the Martinez name, Luis could deal with any problem he ran into.

Risking his life for her... It made no sense. Why would a man who felt the utmost contempt for her, put his life on the line to get the bus she'd requested? He could probably snap his fingers and people would fall in to do his bidding. It made no sense at all.

Shontelle found the fresh clothes she wanted and changed into them, glad to feel clean from the inside out. Not that she looked any different, except for wearing a dark green shirt with the Amigos Tours logo, instead of red. She gave her hair a quick brush, plaited it, and felt considerably better, more equipped to handle whatever came.

Having checked the suite in case anything had been left lying around, she took her bags down to the foyer and left them in Alan's care. "Breakfast," she said and zipped off to the dining room. Maybe by tonight she might feel up to fielding sensitive questions, but she felt too raw to start answering them now.

Most of the tour group was moving out of the dining room as she entered it. Time was getting short. She exchanged quick greetings and hurried to the buffet bar, not that she had suddenly found an appetite but sheer practicality dictated she replenish her energy.

Having picked up a fruit juice, a couple of bread rolls, some slices of cold meat and cheese, she headed for an empty table, not wanting to be drawn into conversation with anyone. The ploy succeeded. She was left to eat her breakfast in peace.

At ten minutes to seven she returned to the foyer to help Alan settle the tour group, answering concerns as best she could and preparing them for the long journey ahead. It was ten hours by road from La Paz to Santa Cruz...if nothing went wrong. Once there, it would be possible to catch a flight to Buenos Aires, then home to Australia.

The mood of the group was jumpy. Those suffering from altitude sickness didn't care what other discomforts they might have to suffer, so long as they were getting away from here. Some were fearful of what lay in wait beyond the hotel.

Australians simply weren't accustomed to a military presence. Apart from a formal parade of war veterans on Anzac Day, soldiers did not feature in their lives, and a tank was only seen in a military museum. There were mutterings of never leaving home again. They had a new appreciation of Australia being called "the lucky country."

The minutes ticked by. A nervous bustle started with people rechecking their luggage, making sure they had everything to hand. Having instructed everyone to stay inside, Alan left them to go out to the street where he could watch for the bus which would have to back in to the cul-de-sac.

Shontelle fixed a patient smile on her face, projecting calm confidence to the group. It took quite a lot of concentration. Her stomach was in knots. As more minutes passed, worries mounted in her mind, becoming impossible to set aside. If the bus didn't come, would that mean something bad had happened to Luis?

Despite the deep hurt he had inflicted on her last night, she did not want him physically injured. She certainly didn't want him dead. Though if he was risking his life by getting the bus for them, it wasn't her fault, was it? It was *his* choice. *He'd* made the deal.

Her mind skipped to what Luis had once told her about his older brother, Eduardo. During the political troubles in Argentina, the military police had simply scooped him up off the street one night, supposedly rounding up young dissidents, and Eduardo was never heard of again, becoming one of the disappeared whose deaths were never recorded.

In Buenos Aires, she had seen for herself the Thursday march of the women now called The Mothers of May, protesting the disappearance of their children. It didn't matter how many years had gone by. They turned up each week to parade their banners with photos in front of Government House because they still had no answers. Rumour had it that many of the lost ones had been taken off by helicopter and dropped in the sea.

Shontelle shivered. Could that happen here in Bolivia? No, surely not. This was a land-locked country, no coastal territory at all. Even if Luis was imprisoned for some reason, Elvira Rosa Martinez had the power to have him freed. Eduardo had probably not been identified before he was killed.

Another dreadful thought hit. What if Luis didn't have time to identify himself? What if some trigger-happy soldier...

Alan burst into the foyer. "It's here!"

Shontelle's knees almost buckled in relief.

"Collect your belongings and come outside now," Alan commanded. "Remember what I said—women to board the bus immediately, men stand ready to load the suitcases in the luggage department. The sooner we get going, the better."

Action seemed to buoy everyone's spirits. There was a buzz of excitement as thirty people headed for the door, carrying their bags. Shontelle lingered behind the rest, ostensibly to check that nothing was left in the foyer. She could see the bus being backed into position in front of the hotel and it *was* Luis in the driver's seat.

Her heart lifted. He was safe. He could return to the Plaza Hotel from here and be absolutely safe. The bus came to a halt, the luggage compartment hatches were unlocked, the door was opened, and Luis rose from the driver's seat. He'd go now, Shontelle thought. This was the last she'd ever see of him.

Strange how torn she felt. Absurd after last night. It shouldn't matter to her. Yet her legs moved faster, wanting to get outside, closer to him before he left. She virtually herded the stragglers of the group past the front door.

Luis was rounding the front of the bus. He saw her at the back of the crowd and for one sizzling moment, their eyes locked. Somehow it was as though everything else ceased to exist and there was only the two of them, tied by a bond that went beyond any other reality. The tug on her heart was so strong, her chest felt ready to burst. Then he tore his gaze away and addressed Alan.

Shontelle was so shaken she could barely put two thoughts together. What did that look from Luis mean? He'd shut the door on her before. There was nothing left of what they'd once shared. Couldn't be.

She tried to collect her scattered wits. Her job was to usher the women onto the bus while Alan supervised the loading of the luggage. Somehow that task fell by the wayside. While she was vaguely aware of the women heading into the bus by themselves, she couldn't drag her attention away from Luis and Alan who were clearly having a tense exchange of words. She walked straight over to them and broke into their conversation.

"Thank you for bringing the bus, Luis," she said with genuine sincerity.

Alan shot her a searing look. "He says he's staying with it."

"Sorry..." She showed her confusion to both of them. "What do you mean?"

"He's not handing it over. He insists on driving it," Alan tersely explained.

"To Santa Cruz?" She looked at Luis in bewilderment.

"To hell and back if necessary," he answered with grim purpose.

"But why?" she cried.

His mouth curled. His dark eyes flashed a derisive gleam at her. "Because you'll be on it, Shontelle. And I'm not finished with you."

She should have said, yes, he was. Or at least said *she* was finished with him. But the words stuck in her throat and she just stared at him, feeling the power of his will swirling around her, tying her to him again. It was crazy. Nothing good could come of this.

They'd scarred each other too badly. Yet the feeling coming from him was different now...not contempt, not dismissal or rejection and certainly not indifference.

"Luis..." Alan started in a tone of protest.

"It's my bus," Luis cut in ruthlessly. "Get your people off it if you won't accept my driving it."

The luggage compartments were being slammed shut. The women were already in their chosen seats and the men were proceeding to join them.

"Goddammit, man! Let my sister go!"

Luis' gaze hadn't shifted from Shontelle's. The black resolution in his eyes was not going to be moved by anything. It was either stay here in La Paz where he would be, as well, or take this journey to Santa Cruz with him. Whichever choice was made, Shontelle knew intuitively Luis did not intend to let her escape him until he *was* finished with her. Whatever that meant.

It certainly wouldn't mean more sex, Shontelle thought with fierce determination. Besides which, on a busload of people she wouldn't be alone with him. Better to let him get his "unfinished" business with her over with in the relative safety of numbers, she decided.

"Better to go with Luis than not go at all, Alan. Everyone's on the bus," she said pointedly. "I'll go and do the head count."

"You can't drive a bus as well as I can, Luis," Alan argued as she moved around them.

"From what I've seen on the streets, you'll have your hands full keeping your people calm," came the grim retort. "This is no picnic trip. You can take over the wheel once we're clear of La Paz."

"So you can have time with Shontelle and tear her into more little pieces."

Already on her way around the front of the bus, Shontelle paused, wishing Alan would keep his mouth shut about her.

"I tell you, it's not right, Luis," he went on. "She hasn't picked herself up from her last affair with you."

"Neither have I, my friend," came the cold reply. "Neither have I."

Shontelle frowned. Was that true?

"What's the point, man? You're never going to marry her. I told her so from the start, but she wouldn't listen."

"*You, too, Alan?*" His voice was ice. "Then some of those pieces can be laid at your door."

"What the hell does that mean?"

"It means stay out of my business on this journey. You don't know a damned thing about what I feel or what I'll do."

Neither did she, Shontelle thought as she moved on to board the bus. It was difficult to focus her attention on completing an accurate head count but everyone had responded to the list of names by the time Alan and Luis had joined them.

Luis took the driver's seat. Alan occupied the tour

guide seat adjacent to it, activating the microphone so the whole group could hear him clearly as he introduced Luis and outlined the planned trip for them. Shontelle settled on the seat left vacant for her, directly behind the driver.

The bus started moving.

She didn't listen to Alan.

The physical trip they were about to take meant nothing to her. It was the journey with Luis that preyed on her mind. What did he want of her now? Where could it lead? How would it end?

CHAPTER NINE

THE streets of La Paz were unnaturally quiet. Traffic was minimal and very few pedestrians were civilians. The eerie sense of moving through a war zone was strong and oppressive. There was no buzz of conversation in the bus. If the passengers spoke at all, it was in whispers.

Shontelle noted that Luis avoided driving along the main thoroughfares, detouring around them through a series of side streets. It was obvious he was highly aware of the danger of being stopped, accelerating past groups of soldiers before they had time to react to a busload of people going by.

Alan instructed the tour group to remain seated naturally, not to duck down or to act in any way which might appear suspicious. Tourists were not targets in the current political conflict. Shontelle hoped her brother was right in his reading of the situation.

They were travelling along what appeared to be a deserted stretch of road, when a tank emerged from a cross-street, directly in their path. Luis had to brake or collide with it. The bus came to a screeching halt and ominously, the tank halted, as well. Slowly, terrifyingly, its turret swung towards them. So did the long barrel of its gun.

Agitation broke out amongst the tour group, screams from the women, shocked cursing from the men.

"Be quiet and sit still!" Alan barked into the microphone.

They settled down but the atmosphere in the bus was thick with fear. The gun did not move. Neither did the tank. Shontelle suddenly realised the barrel was trained directly on Luis. Her mind was jolted into two quick leaps—the driver—who had the colouring of a local man.

She was out of her seat instantly, throwing her arms around Luis' neck, and lowering her head next to his so her fair hair could be seen. She was so clearly not a native South American, it seemed logical that whoever was sighting them from the tank would have second thoughts about attacking them.

"Shontelle..." Alan started to protest.

"Luis is dark, Alan. Could be taken for a Bolivian. Show yourself. Tell them we're tourists and we have sick people on board."

"Right! Open the door, Luis."

Alan waved at the tank to draw attention to himself as he rose from his seat. Luis activated the door. It hissed open.

"Stay near the bus, Alan," Luis sharply advised. "Don't look threatening."

The next few minutes were extremely tense. Alan stood just outside the door, waving and explaining in a quick stream of Spanish. No verbal reply came from the occupants of the tank. Alan kept talking, emphasising Australia and foreign relations.

The gun started to move, swinging back to the direction the tank had originally been taking. Then the tank started to move, proceeding on its route, unblocking their way forward. The relief in the bus was palpable. Alan jumped back on board. Some of the group cheered him, grateful that the crisis was past. Shontelle belatedly realised she was still hanging on to Luis and started to withdraw her arms.

He caught her right hand, his strong fingers wrapping around hers, squeezing, transmitting a quick jolt of electric heat. It lasted only a moment or two before release came. Other actions had to be carried out, closing the door, getting the bus moving again. There was no glance, no word, just that quick squeeze, then total concentration on the job of driving them out of La Paz.

Alan clapped her on the shoulder. "Good thinking," he said with a wide grin, the zest of having won this round beaming from his face.

She nodded and returned to her seat.

Alan gave a morale-boosting speech over the microphone but Shontelle didn't listen to it. She stared down at the hand Luis had gripped, using her other hand to stroke away the feeling of his touch. Her mind fretted over how strongly he could still affect her. It was as though somehow he was imprinted on her—mind, body and soul—and it was an indelible imprint she couldn't wipe out no matter how hard she tried.

He touched her and instantly triggered a chemical reaction through her entire body. How could he do that after last night? And the look he had given her earlier—just one look—and she was drawn to him. Fatal attraction, she thought bitterly.

But she would not let him take her again. If he wanted something more from her it had to be on a very different basis. Respect, for a start. And the truth had to be told from both sides...no more prideful holding back. She recalled Luis' fierce words to Alan...

You don't know a damned thing about what I feel or what I'll do.

One thing he wouldn't do, Shontelle vowed to herself, was seduce her into accepting him as her lover again. Her jaw firmed in resolution. He would not shake her on that.

Then she silently laughed at herself. Unfinished business didn't have to mean sex. It more likely meant getting his facts straight. Then he could move on, satisfied he knew where all the pieces fitted. And maybe the same knowledge would help her put this in the past, as well.

The bus was almost at the top of the long hill that led to the airport, though it was not their destination. They had to go past it to get out of La Paz and on their way to Santa Cruz. However, the area around the airport was sure to be heavily guarded. Alan had anticipated there might be trouble there, if anywhere.

He'd already underestimated possible problems, Shontelle thought, tensing in readiness for more as Luis drove past groups of soldiers who eyed the bus suspiciously. Military jeeps were parked alongside the road but none of them gave chase. It seemed like a miracle when they actually cleared the whole stretch past the airport without being stopped.

The tour group started to relax as the bus travelled on through the settlements on the outskirts of the city. People made jokes to lighten the atmosphere and an air of triumphant jollity started to develop. Alan told a couple of stories about tight spots he'd been in during other tours, making the escapes sound amusing. It really seemed the danger was past—behind them. The bus moved into open country, safely on their journey.

No one was thinking about the farmers' revolt.

At least, Shontelle wasn't. Her gaze was trained on the man sitting in front of her. She saw what Luis saw just as he spoke.

"Alan...ahead of us!"

Large groups of men were milling around what appeared to be a huge speed bump spread across the road.

"They've dug a trench," Luis said, no doubt at all about what the hump meant.

Shontelle's heart sank. A speed bump was passable, but a trench?

"Put your foot down, Luis," Alan advised quickly. "We'll have to jump it."

"No telling how wide it is," came the terse warning.

"If you don't want to risk your bus..."

"Prepare your people." It was a grim command.

"Men, up on your feet and put all the overhead hand luggage under seats or on the floor," Alan yelled, clapping his hands to encourage fast action. "The farmers have dug a trench across the road. Our driver is speeding up and we're going to be airborne to cross it. Move, move...we don't want any injuries from flying bags."

The acceleration in speed made the task more difficult but it was accomplished in a wildly lurching fashion. The hump hiding the trench was coming up very fast and looking bigger by the second. Which could mean the gap in the road behind it was too wide. Shontelle started praying it wasn't. This gamble could end in a very nasty accident.

"Sit, sit!" Alan yelled. "Brace yourselves in your seats for impact when we land on the other side..."

If, Shontelle thought darkly.

"...Anyone with a bad back, try to cushion yourself against the thump."

Silence, except for the rustle of adjustments and much heavy breathing. They were hurtling towards the crisis point. Shontelle wondered what Luis was thinking. Why was he risking so much? What was at stake for him?

He stood up behind the wheel, bracing himself against his seat. Could he see beyond the hump? Impossible to stop now anyway. Was he regretting the risk he'd accepted? He'd be the first hit if the trench was too wide. Luis and Alan...*then me,* Shontelle realised. It could all end here and she'd never know...

The thought stopped there.

The bus hit the heaped pile of rubble dug from the trench and lifted, slightly skewing in the air from an uneven take-off. Shontelle looked frantically out the side window. The gap... Oh, God! Oh, God! It was too big...but the bus was soaring, reaching over the threatening maw of emptiness below them. They weren't going to crash into it. As the long vehicle started dipping forward on the other side, it shot through Shontelle's mind that the back wheels weren't going to make it across.

The front of the bus landed at an angle, half facing towards an open field. The left rear end wheel caught the trench but the right side made it onto the road. With a heart-stopping, wrenching manoeuvre, Luis somehow got enough traction to drag the trapped wheel out. The bus careered down the road in a wild zigzag as he fought for control of it, every muscle stretched to the task.

Shontelle was very, very glad there weren't any roadside trees or other obstacles, and no bends to ne-gotiate—just a straight road and unfenced fields on either side. Hand luggage was sliding all over the floor. There were grunts and groans as the passengers were knocked around, but no one screamed. Shontelle felt they were all fiercely willing Luis to pull them through this nightmare.

How long it took she had no idea, but he finally did it, slowing the bus down, gradually easing it to a very ragged halt. The cessation of movement brought a shock of disbelief. It was hard to take in that it was actually over and they'd made it intact.

"Back left wheel's locked up, Alan," Luis muttered.

He jumped up from his seat. "I'll go and have a look."

The door whooshed open as Luis said, "I'll come with you."

Alan flashed him a grin. "Great driving, man!"

"Born to survive," Luis retorted wryly.

"Shontelle, take over in here," Alan instructed.

"Will do." She rose shakily to her feet.

Luis paused, dark eyes sharply scanning hers. He said nothing to her, just gave a curt nod before following Alan outside. *She* should have said something, Shontelle thought crossly. At least thanked him. But the moment was gone and she had no idea what the look and nod from him had meant. Satisfaction that she was more or less fighting fit?

This was no time to concern herself about it. Moving quickly she picked up the microphone and turned to address the tour group.

"Is everyone okay?"

It stirred them all into taking stock of themselves. They reported probably a few bruises but no cuts or other injuries.

"How much more of this can we expect?" the chief trouble-maker in the group demanded.

"I don't know," Shontelle answered truthfully.

"Damned madness! Alan shouldn't have led us…"

"Now, hold it a minute, Ron," another cut in. "Alan gave us fair warning there could be trouble. You were the one who insisted he get us out of La Paz or you'd badmouth his tours when you got home, remember?"

"Yeah!" another chimed in. "Better keep your mouth shut, Ron. You not only asked for this, you roped us all into supporting you. We're here now with no broken bones so far. We've got no complaint. Right?"

"Besides, what an adventure to tell our grandchildren!" one of the women said, awed at having lived through the experience.

"Wish I could have videoed it all," another remarked with rueful humour.

Rebellion over, Shontelle thought with considerable relief. "Well, if you feel up to it," she began cautiously, "it would be a good idea to reorganise the loose hand luggage on the floor while Alan and Luis are fixing the wheel."

"Can they fix it?" someone asked.

"Alan's a highly skilled mechanic. He'll get us going again," Shontelle answered confidently.

The assurance encouraged people to start hunting for their belongings and securing them in a more orderly fashion than they'd had time to do so beforehand. The sound of hammering underneath the back of the bus started and continued while the interior tidy-up was in progress.

Shontelle wondered if Luis and Alan were settling some of their differences as they worked together. She hoped some of the hostility would be eased. Fighting Luis was difficult enough without having to fight her brother, as well.

One of the women suggested opening the thermoses provided by the hotel and having cups of coffee.

Shontelle vetoed the idea. They weren't so far away from the aggressive gathering of farmers to be complacent about time. They had to be off again, the moment Luis and Alan finished the repairs. Apart from which, they were barely an hour's journey out of La Paz. They had nine more hours on the road before they reached Santa Cruz.

No one protested.

At last the hammering stopped. Everyone perked up as Alan and Luis boarded the bus again...everyone except Shontelle. She immediately tensed, glancing warily at the two men's faces. Alan was obviously in high good humour. Her brother seemed to thrive on danger. Luis' expression was more guarded but she sensed a radiation of energy that put her nerves even more on edge.

Alan took the microphone from her. "Any problems?" he asked quietly.

She shook her head and he waved her back to her seat. Luis moved to the instrument panel and activated the closing of the door.

"Okay, we're about to roll again," Alan announced. "We'll travel for two more hours before stopping for..." he smiled "...a refreshment opportunity. If anyone develops an urgent problem before then, let me know. I'll be taking over the driving now. Luis' muscles need a bit of relaxation..."

Shontelle frowned. Had Luis pulled something? He hadn't shown any strain in his movements.

"How about giving him a clap for a fantastic job of getting us this far in one piece?" Alan suggested, starting off the applause.

Everyone joined in enthusiastically. Luis turned around and acknowledged them with a casual salute and a dry little smile. Alan set aside the microphone and took the driver's seat. The two men had a brief, private discussion. Then Alan gunned the motor and the bus started moving, in a straight line, much to Shontelle's relief. The back wheel problem had obviously been fixed.

She expected Luis to take Alan's seat, but he didn't. Without so much as a by-your-leave, he stepped back and settled himself onto the twin passenger seat beside her.

Every nerve in Shontelle's body jangled. Her hands clenched. She almost cringed away from him in fear of being touched. Which was ridiculous, she fiercely told herself. What could Luis do to her here in front of a busload of people? She was safe from any unwelcome touching. Alan was directly within call, too. Not that she wanted to involve him. She could cope with Luis by herself. Of course she could.

"Are you hurt?" she asked brusquely, not quite able to bring herself to look directly at him.

"No," he answered.

"Then why aren't you driving?"

"Because I want time with you."

Her heart squeezed tight. "Did Alan agree to this?"

"Yes."

Two hours, she thought, staring at the back of her brother's head. Was he listening? No, concentrating on the road, she decided. The drone of the engine was probably filling his ears, as well. The cushioned backrests of their seats closed them off from the passengers behind them. This was probably as good a place as any for a private talk.

Shontelle steeled herself to look at the man who had given her so much torment. Slowly she turned her head, met his waiting gaze, and at point-blank range, asked, "Why?"

The dark eyes had a black intensity of purpose that sent shivers down her spine. "Tell me about your meeting with my mother."

The words "my mother" were edged with acid.

Shontelle wrenched her gaze away, deeply disturbed by the force of energy he emitted. "Why dig around in the past?" she cried. "What point is there now?"

"As far as I'm concerned, the past is the present. And I shall deal with it," he stated with ruthless intent.

Shontelle shook her head, not wanting to relive the pain of Elvira Martinez's disclosures. "You deceived me two years ago, Luis," she accused bitterly.

"No. I didn't."

The rebuttal was instant and powerfully stark.

Shontelle closed her eyes. She couldn't bear it if he was telling the truth. She just couldn't bear it.

"Start talking, Shontelle," he commanded. "Tell me every detail of your experience with my mother."

Again the acid emphasis on "my mother" as though he was barely suppressing a violent flow of bitterness.

The truth, she thought. However much it hurt, whatever it might mean to her, she had to know it, too. So she cast her mind back to that fatal day...the day Elvira Rosa Martinez broke her heart and changed the course of her life...and started to recall it in all its painful detail.

CHAPTER TEN

Two years had not faded the memory of her meeting with Elvira Rosa Martinez. Shontelle had tried to seal it into a hidden compartment in her mind, but once the locked doors were opened up, it flooded out so vividly, it could have been yesterday...visually, emotionally, physically.

"You said it was the day before you left me," Luis prompted.

"Yes. But it didn't really start then," Shontelle answered slowly, remembering back to the weeks they'd spent together, living in Luis' apartment which was wonderfully well situated in the Barrio Recoleta. This was considered the most chic neighbourhood in Buenos Aires and Shontelle had been more than happy to call it home. Except Luis kept his life there strictly separate from his *family* home which was only a short distance away from the apartment.

"My mother had contacted you beforehand?" he asked sharply.

"No. But you avoided introducing me to her. You also avoided introducing me to any of your friends or social acquaintances in Buenos Aires." She turned to search his eyes. "Why was that, Luis?"

He held her gaze unflinchingly. "I didn't want to share you."

"Did you ever plan to?"

He shrugged. "It would have become inevitable if you'd stayed."

"Were you ashamed of me?"

He frowned. "Whatever for?"

"Not measuring up in some way."

His eyes flashed black venom. "Are these my mother's words?"

"If you had not decided to keep me to yourself, her words wouldn't have had any power, Luis."

She turned her head away and stared blindly out the side window, remembering how she'd filled in all those days he'd spent at the Martinez company offices, working long hours. She'd filled them alone. No companions. Just waiting out the time until Luis came back to her.

Admittedly it had not been difficult. There was so much to do and enjoy; roaming around the famous and fascinating Recoleta cemetery where Eva Peron had finally been laid to rest, wandering around the plazas, watching the mime artists, listening to mini-concerts by street buskers, looking through galleries. Buenos Aires was called the Paris of the Americas for good reason. Even the architecture was fascinating.

She hadn't been bored.

Not at all.

But she had been alone. In a strange country. In a

strange culture. Even so, she hadn't felt really *foreign* until the day with Luis' mother. And Claudia Gallardo.

"You know…one of the hardest things to bear that day was her sympathy," Shontelle dryly remarked. "How sorry she was that I'd been so blind about what your relationship with me meant. How very wrong it was for her son to have deceived me about my place in his life."

"What place was that…according to my mother?"

"Oh, good for satisfying the desires men have. Not good enough to marry, of course," she answered flippantly. "Women like me get *used* so the fine men of Argentina can behave themselves with the properly brought up virgins they marry."

"You believed I had so little honour I would use a woman—any woman—*let alone the sister of a friend,* for such a purpose?" he bit out scathingly.

She swung fiercely condemning eyes on him. "You used me as a whore last night. Are you going to deny that?"

"You had a choice," he retaliated, hard black eyes denying any shame in his actions. "You chose the role. The same role you put me in two years ago. Someone to be used for sexual satisfaction."

"You were never that to me," she cried. "I only said so because…"

"Because my mother's words meant more to you than all we'd been to each other?" he interpreted savagely.

"Not just *words,* Luis," she retorted just as savagely. "I met your bride-to-be, Claudia Gallardo."

"Ah…" His eyes glittered. "Did Claudia actually say she was my fiancée?"

"Betrothed was the word used."

"By Claudia?"

Shontelle frowned. She couldn't recall Claudia actually saying she was betrothed to Luis, yet everything she said and did had certainly implied it. "*When I am married to Luis*…it was a kind of refrain she tossed at me over lunch, prefacing her plans for the future with you," she related, determined on being accurate in her recollections. "It was your mother who used *betrothed.* Before Claudia arrived."

"Where was this lunch?"

"At your family home in the Avenue Alvear."

His jaw visibly tightened. His lips compressed into a thin line. She felt an emanation of wild, destructive violence before he brought it under control.

"How did this come about?" he demanded, his voice thick with the unresolved conflicts inside him.

"Your mother came to the apartment that morning," she replied quickly. "It was about nine-thirty. She introduced herself and invited me…" A wave of nausea shot bile up Shontelle's throat. She swallowed hard and turned her head away from the sickening lack of sympathy in Luis' eyes. "…To learn more about you and your life," she added dully.

This was hopeless…hopeless… No good was going to come from raking over the past. She tried to focus on the present, the journey they were on now. Alan was driving fast across the high Andean plateau. At least the weather wouldn't hold them up, Shontelle thought. It couldn't be a finer, sunnier day.

Like the day Elvira Rosa Martinez had walked into her life.

Alan had told her Luis' family was very wealthy. He had listed off their assets when he had grown concerned over her involvement with his friend. Though all the time she had spent with Luis, his wealth hadn't really seemed relevant to her. He hadn't pushed it in her face.

The boat he'd hired for their trip down the Amazon was more like *The African Queen* than a luxury cruiser. His apartment had certainly been comfortable, but not what she'd call showy. It wasn't until she'd opened the door to the woman who introduced herself as his mother that she saw serious wealth being flaunted.

Beautifully coiffeured black hair was artfully winged with white. The deep mulberry-coloured suit was very smartly trimmed with black, its classy elegance marking it as an Italian design, most probably Cerruti. Shoes and handbag were black with a mulberry trim, obviously made to complement the clothes.

Having toured the H. Stern workshops in Rio de Janeiro, Shontelle recognised the work of the famous jeweler in the fabulous geometric design of the woman's necklace and earrings; hexagonal wine-red rubellites set in yellow and black gold, costing a small fortune. The rings on her hands were equally fabulous.

Shontelle had instantly felt like a waif from the streets, wearing merely a loose button-through cotton dress designed more to hide a traveller's pouch for money and passport than to flatter her figure or give her a bit of style. The sandals on her feet were for practical comfort.

However, since her touring wardrobe did not contain fancy clothes, she had to accept her own appearance as being as good as it could be in the circumstances. Luis had never once criticised it. Though she'd thought afterwards he liked her best naked, anyway.

The plush chauffeur-driven car she'd been led to had made her feel even more self-conscious. The distance they travelled was easily walkable, a matter of a few blocks, but Shontelle was acutely aware that walking the streets with the common people was not the done thing in Elvira Rosa Martinez's world. They drove right to her front door, a semicircular driveway guarded by huge iron gates allowing this private access.

Front door was a misnomer for the huge, elaborate portico that embellished the entrance to a home which was far more than a home. It was probably impossible to explain to Luis, who'd grown up with it, how overwhelming that virtual palace in Alvear Street had been to her, the almost obscene wealth evident in every room she'd been shown, furnishings and furniture imported from Spain, Italy, France. The ballroom had featured all the unbelievable richness of the hall of mirrors in Versailles, reflecting over and over again how hopelessly unsuitable Shontelle looked in such a place.

Naturally, Elvira Rosa Martinez was far too gracious to say so. She didn't have to. Pointing out family heirlooms and portraits, recounting the achievements of Martinez generations in Argentina, she'd made it subtly clear to Shontelle that Luis had the responsibility of carrying on a heritage—an integral part of him no foreigner could even begin to comprehend.

Beside her, Luis stirred from his tense stillness, thrusting out his hand in an impatient gesture. "So tell me the judgment you made...of my *real life*."

Shontelle sighed at his persistence. "You know it better than I, Luis."

"A conducted tour through the mausoleum must have been quite an experience for you," he went on sardonically. "All my forebears framed on the walls, the accumulated treasures of centuries of plunder and exploitation on ostentatious display. I'm sure my mother didn't spare you anything."

His disrepectful tone startled Shontelle. She glanced sharply at him. "Don't you value what's yours?"

His eyes mocked the value she'd placed on it. "It

cost too much. Did Claudia join you for the grand exhibition?''

"No.''

Shontelle scooped in a deep breath as that memory billowed into her mind—the perfectly presented Claudia wearing a spectacular silk dress in glorious autumn tones, highlighting her lovely, glowing olive skin, a lustrous fall of black curly hair, and dark velvet eyes. Fine gold chains and a gold filigree necklace and earrings added their rich touch to her young vibrancy. It was all too obvious she belonged to the same class that the Martinez home portrayed so tellingly.

"Claudia arrived about midday,'' she added, anticipating Luis' next question and deciding she might as well satisfy his curiosity and have done with it.

"Were you introduced to her as my secret mistress?''

A surge of hot blood scorched up her neck and flooded into her cheeks. She shook her head, trying to get rid of the painful flush. "Your mother tactfully explained about your friendship with Alan and simply introduced me as Alan's sister who was staying in Buenos Aires for a while.''

"Tactful!'' Luis snorted derisively. "That was for your benefit, Shontelle, not Claudia's. Who was clearly in on the game of getting you out of my life.''

Was that true? Even if it was, didn't Claudia have good reason to want to be rid of the woman sharing Luis' bed…his *secret mistress?* Having just returned from a tour of Europe, it must have been galling to hear that her man had been playing fast and loose with another woman.

Though the comments she had made over lunch about her future with Luis had seemed quite natural, artless. Impossible to tell if they were or not now. They had certainly robbed Shontelle of any appetite…any appetite for food, for staying with Luis, for remaining in Buenos Aires any longer than it took to get a flight home to Australia. The feeling was so sickeningly strong that she didn't belong with these people and never would.

She remembered staring at the centrepiece on the dining table, a magnificently crafted artwork in silver. It was a tree rising from a mound of grass and roots where three deer lay at rest. At the top of the trunk was a holder from which spread a beautiful array of fresh red roses, forming the foliage of the tree. Similarly, silver branches held other, smaller holders, containing more bunches of roses. The effect was stunningly sumptuous and the scent of the roses dreadfully insidious. Red roses for love. Shontelle had hated red roses ever since.

"Was Claudia wearing a ring on the third finger of her left hand?" Luis asked.

"No. Though she talked about what she fancied. An oval yellow diamond surrounded by two rows of white diamonds."

Louis muttered something vicious under his breath.

The Spanish was too fast or too colloquial for Shontelle to pick up the meaning.

"Yet even hearing all this," he said tersely, "you were still there for me in the apartment that evening."

"I didn't want to believe you'd used me like that. I thought there was a chance you had changed your mind about marrying Claudia," she explained ruefully.

"Then why did you not speak of this?"

Because it was too shaming if it was true. Because she still wanted him. Because she simply couldn't face it...until after the telephone call.

She heaved a sigh to ease the burden of all she'd felt, and still felt. "Your mother called you that evening. At the apartment. She said she'd call at eight o'clock. And she did, didn't she, Luis?"

"Yes."

"With an invitation for you to bring me to her next Sunday lunch."

"No," he answered vehemently.

"Luis, I heard the excuse you made. In fact, you sounded extremely vexed and impatient with her for suggesting it."

"She wanted me to be Claudia's escort at a welcome home party. It had nothing to do with you, Shontelle. Nothing!" He gave a derisive laugh. "Or so I thought at the time. I actually thought you were still safe from her. Safe! *¡Madre de Dios!*"

Confusion swallowed up Shontelle's understanding

of the situation. Was Luis afraid of his mother? How much power did Elvira have over him?

"My mother planned this call with you...as a test of my intentions?" he probed in a hard ruthless tone.

She gave him her vision of the situation because she had nothing else to give him. "I thought it was a woman to woman thing. A kindness to show me where I stood with you."

"So when you heard my negative reply, you assumed this meant I was keeping you as my secret mistress...yes?" he snapped.

"Yes," she acknowledged.

"And the fire of your love for me went out that night."

She'd cravenly given herself one last night with him, but had found it impossible to respond to his lovemaking, impossible to block Claudia out of her mind, impossible to feel Luis really loved her.

"I felt...used," she repeated wearily.

"So you made me feel *used*."

"Yes."

"For you, it was marriage or nothing."

He had no right to leap to that conclusion. Her love had been freely given, no strings attached. "We hadn't got that far, Luis," she angrily reminded him.

"No, we hadn't. Which was why I did not throw you into the ring with my mother who had her own plans for me."

"You must have known of them," Shontelle argued. "There was too much...too much evidence."

His hands sliced the air in a contemptuous scissor movement. "Talk. Deliberate, divisive talk. If you had spoken to me...but no, you decided I would marry Claudia and there would be nothing for us."

"Back then...your marriage to Claudia meant there was nothing for *me,* Luis," she fiercely corrected him. "Nothing I could feel happy with."

"Claudia Gallardo will never get her yellow diamond from me! Not from *me!* Never!" he declared passionately. "I see now she is every bit as manipulative as my mother and I will not be caught in either of their webs."

Shontelle retreated into silence. She had never been part of this *power* side of Luis' life. From what he'd said, it seemed now that she'd been a victim of it, but it was all beyond her experience.

The old saying...*power corrupts*...slid into her mind. It had never applied to her personal life. She didn't want it to, either. It felt dark and ugly. Luis had accused her of having no faith, no trust, but how could anything be trusted or believed in Luis' world if his own mother plotted behind his back?

The truth—if that was what she had now—did not give her any satisfaction. Only sadness.

Alan had been right.

Her relationship with Luis had been doomed from the start.

Love didn't always find a way.

Not when there was too much stacked against it.

CHAPTER ELEVEN

Luis closed his eyes. He felt like a drowning man whose whole life was passing before him. And there was no rescue to be had. No going back to a more promising place. He'd killed any possibility of that last night.

The rage inside him was futile. What was done could not be undone. Shontelle—the Shontelle who had brought love and joy and laughter and the sweetest of pleasures into his life—was forever lost to him. No point in blaming her for it. She'd been an innocent, mangled by the forces that had ruled his world, forces he'd known all too well and had wanted to ignore with her. To be free of them with her.

Fool! he thought savagely.

He might have won her back last night. Instead, he'd driven her further away. Beyond reach now. He could feel the shield she'd wrapped around herself, blocking him out. And why not? He was pain...pain in all its forms.

He'd done wrong by Alan, too. Another innocent party. While the guilty ones had almost reaped the benefits of their self-serving conspiracy. Tonight, if there'd been no trouble in La Paz, he would have presented Claudia with the yellow diamond ring, and his mother would have beamed triumphant approval over the proceedings.

How the coin of Fate turns, he thought with an acute sense of irony. But for Alan's need for a bus, his mother would have succeeded in her drive to link the Gallardo and Martinez fortunes. He would have let her succeed, and in doing so, would have provided her with justification for sacrificing the one great love of his life. For that, there was no justification. None that Luis would ever accept.

Everything Shontelle had said to him last night made sense now. If he hadn't been so blinded by bitterness he might have picked up on her repeated references to marriage, questioned more closely.

No...on reflection, there'd been no chance of his being sensitive to what was going on in her mind. The damage had been well and truly done two years ago. Old scars didn't suddenly clear up. But those who'd delivered the wounds could and would still pay for the injuries.

The beautifully polished, submissive Claudia, offering her cold comfort, hiding a Machiavellian heart...she could kiss goodbye to whatever ambitions she'd nursed as an outcome of their marriage merger. The sly bitch hadn't turned a hair at making Shontelle bleed, delivering her poisonous little cuts. He could see her delicately picking through her lunch, sticking her knife in with sweet, loving smiles. She, who didn't know a damned thing about love. Not the kind of love Shontelle...

His heart cramped.

Forget it, he railed at himself. Alan was right. Let it go. God knew there were other things that had to be dealt with. Like his mother...

If only Eduardo had not been taken...Luis could mark the change in his mother from that terrible grief. Not even his father's death, five years before Eduardo's, had touched her so deeply, so traumatically. Perhaps because there'd been no body to bury, no answers to be drawn from anyone.

It was then that the woman she was today had emerged. Control had become everything. The more wealth she acquired, the more power she had, the more control she wielded. Loving anyone was a weakness that left one vulnerable. Better not to love. Better to hold what you had with an iron fist and never risk it, never allow even the possibility of risking it. Protect. Shore up the walls so they were impregnable. Keep a constant watch.

She didn't put her philosophy in such stark terms, but that was what it boiled down to. Luis had fought it for years, to no avail. She'd hung his heritage—Eduardo's heritage—around his neck like an albatross, and wouldn't listen to any point of view that differed from hers. He'd understood—to a degree—what drove her. He'd tried to fill the void she feared—within reason. But for her to take Shontelle out of his life with such ruthless efficiency, uncaring of the pain she gave to either of them...

She had to be stopped.

So forcefully she would never interfere in his life again.

Better still, if she could be made to realise how far she'd gone along a road that was intolerable to him, maybe she could be turned around. Shutting her out of his life was not the answer. She'd find a way to intrude, to interfere. She had to be faced with consequences she couldn't change.

But how to do it? How to hammer it home?

He knew what he wanted to do, what he'd love to do, but he also knew in his bones Shontelle wouldn't agree to it. She was probably longing for him to move away from her right now, have nothing more to do with him.

Yet he couldn't let the idea go. It was the perfect act of justice. No secret moves. No sly manoeuvrings. An act no one could stop, a public act in the spotlight of his mother's own choosing, an undeniable act that declared Luis Angel Martinez his *own man* against any force that could be rallied against him.

But he needed Shontelle's cooperation. Would she listen? Would she see it was an act of justice for her, too? Her response would almost certainly be she wanted no more to do with either him or his family. But it was worth a try. It was very much worth a try. It might just balance the scales so that Shontelle would look at him and see a man she could love again, a man who was free to love.

CHAPTER TWELVE

ALAN made good time to Caracollo, their first stopping place. To have achieved this distance without further mishap put everyone in a good mood.

"You have twenty minutes maximum," Alan warned. "Don't wander away. Use the facilities you'll find across the road, then come back to the bus. Shontelle and I will have coffee and cake and soft drinks ready for you."

The tour group alighted from the bus looking both relieved and happy. Shontelle was grateful for the opportunity to move away from Luis and get about her business of helping Alan with the refreshments. To her frustration, Luis offered his assistance, as well, hovering around her until everything was set up. She refused to look at him, knowing it would only upset her. She was tense enough as it was, feeling him watching her.

Maybe the message that his presence was unwelcome finally got through to him. He drew out a compact mobile telephone that had been clipped to his belt and walked away to make whatever calls he wanted to make in private. Shontelle insisted to herself she was not curious about them. Luis' life was

104

no business of hers anymore. She was better off out of it.

"Are you okay?" Alan asked.

"Yes," she answered shortly.

"I was wrong about Luis, Shontelle. Sorry for thinking I knew better."

"Don't worry about it. We were all wrong. About a lot of things."

"Did you sort it out?"

"Yes."

"And?"

"And nothing. There's nowhere to go."

Alan frowned, not liking the answer, but people were trailing back to the bus and his attention was claimed by them. Shontelle's attention, too.

Cochabamba was their next stop, then the long stretch through the lowlands to Santa Cruz, hopefully arriving there by early evening. Alan had booked them into a hotel for the night, and on a flight to Buenos Aires tomorrow morning. All going well, they would arrive there in time to make the prebooked flight home to Australia. All going well...which it rarely did in South America. Keeping schedules ran on hope, never certainty.

A downpour of rain could block roads, holding up traffic for hours. Flights were cancelled or delayed with no apology or explanation. A gunfight had broken out in Rio on this trip, causing them to take a long detour around the trouble spot. Then a political upheaval in La Paz. Hopefully that problem was behind them, but who knew what they'd run into next?

On the other side of the ledger, was the sheer magic of this continent, so many incredible wonders: La Paz itself, with its fantastic Moon Valley, the Inca history in Cuzco and the strange, eerie atmosphere of the abandoned city of Machu Picchu, the splendid primaeval spectacle of the Iguazu Falls, the awesome Amazon Valley, the beauty of Rio with its Sugarloaf Mountain and the majestic statue of Christ the Redeemer, Buenos Aires...where the Martinez family lived.

Shontelle tried to sigh away the pain.

Whatever discomforts their tour groups ran into on tour, the trip was always worthwhile, the journey truly memorable. Especially this one, Shontelle thought wryly as they herded everyone back on the bus. She suggested to Alan she do a tour commentary over the microphone during this next leg of the trip.

"It will keep them entertained," she pressed, wanting to avoid sitting with Luis again.

Alan surprised her by replying, "I'll do it myself. Luis said he'd take the wheel to Cochabamba. We'll get along faster and more safely with us both coming fresh to driving after a spell."

So Luis *was* letting it go.

It was the inevitable outcome, Shontelle told herself, as they got under way again. She sat alone, which should have relieved the stress of being constantly aware of him, but now she found herself staring at the back of his head, wishing she could read his thoughts. The stress didn't diminish at all. She gradually sank into a black pit of depression.

No heart...no faith...no trust...

The words Luis had hurled at her earlier this morning kept pounding through her mind, making her head ache. She ached all over. The plain truth was she hadn't believed enough in his love for her. She'd let her own sense of inadequacy swallow it up, then spit it out. She had trusted his mother instead of Luis, put her faith in women she didn't know against the man she did know. He was right. Where was the heart in that?

Broken, she thought. Smashed. Bleeding to death.

And there was no cure for it. None at all.

Eventually they reached Cochabamba and stopped for lunch. Luis went off by himself, the mobile telephone in his hand ready to make more calls. Probably shuffling his business affairs around, Shontelle thought. She and Alan led the tour group into a hotel where a buffet spread provided instant self-service. Once everyone was fed and watered, it was back to the bus.

The next stretch of their journey to Villa Tunari was very picturesque and again Shontelle offered to carry on a commentary, aware that Alan would be doing this drive.

"Better to keep quiet and let them doze after lunch," he argued. "Let's save it for when they get restless later on."

Which meant she had to sit with Luis.

More torture.

She shrank into herself as best she could as he settled beside her. Anticipating a long journey of tense silence, she was surprised when he spoke to her, the moment Alan had the bus moving.

"Will you accept an apology for my behaviour last night, Shontelle?"

She glanced sharply at him, drawn more by the low intense tone than the question. There was no mockery in his eyes, not one trace of contempt for her, just deep unfathomable darkness. His face looked strained, absolutely serious. Shontelle's heart skittered nervously. Had she been wrong about his decision to let it all go?

"We've both acted regrettably, Luis," she answered stiffly. "I'm sorry, too, for the pain I caused you."

His mouth twisted into a rueful grimace. "Saying *sorry* isn't enough, is it?"

She shook her head. "There are too many other factors."

"Yes," he agreed.

They were in tune with each other on that score, Shontelle thought, sliding back into bleak despondency.

"My mother is holding a grand reception tonight," he remarked. "The guest list includes the most prominent people in Argentina. The Gallardo family will certainly be there. In strength."

Shontelle fiercely wished he'd keep his family business to himself.

"I would be very honoured," he went on, "if you'd be my partner to this highly glittering occasion, Shontelle."

Shock addled her brains. He couldn't mean it. She was either dreaming or he'd taken leave of his senses. Yet he still looked perfectly serious.

"Why?" she blurted out, needing to sort through the ambivalence of such a suggestion.

His mouth curved into a whimsical little smile. "It is, perhaps, one thing I can right, out of all the wrongs I've done you."

"How could that make anything right?" she cried.

"Two years ago, I made you feel less than you were, Shontelle," he said quietly. "It was unintentional, but a very grave error on my part. I would like, at least, to correct that error. I'd be very proud to present you as my partner in front of my mother and all of Argentina."

Shontelle squirmed in anguish. "It's too late for that, Luis."

"No. It's never too late to give due respect. To restore pride and self-esteem. I shall do it tonight, if you'll allow me."

"It doesn't matter. These people are not part of my life. They never will be."

His face hardened. "It doesn't matter that they lied to you? That they lied about me to make you feel like *nothing?* You can forgive and forget that, Shontelle? Or will it not always burn a hole in your heart?''

"It's in the past, Luis.''

"No." His eyes blazed with passionate intensity. "The past is never in the past. It lives with us. Always. I need…please, I beg you…let me give you justice.''

She wrenched her gaze from his, feeling the power of his will tugging on hers, intent on drawing her with him again. For what? Justice was a cold repast. It could never give back what had been taken. At best, all it did was balance the scales.

Nevertheless, there was an insidious attraction about turning up at a grand reception given by Elvira Rosa Martinez, being flaunted as Luis' chosen partner for the evening, right under his mother's and Claudia Gallardo's snobbish noses. Yes, there would be some satisfaction in that…robbing them of their mean triumph over her.

But it would also mean more time spent with Luis…time filled with painful might-have-beens. He'd be touching her, stirring memories, putting her through a make-believe situation, pretending all was right between them when it wasn't. She couldn't do it.

Besides, how did he expect to get to this reception? "Have you forgotten we're in the middle of Bolivia, Luis? We'll be lucky to make it to Santa Cruz tonight.''

"A company jet will be waiting there to fly us on to Buenos Aires."

She looked at him in astonishment. "You've already made arrangements?"

"For me, yes. I hope you will accompany me."

His calls on the mobile telephone, Shontelle thought, and wondered when he had started planning this proposition. As early as before Caracollo, or had the idea grown on him while he drove to Cochabamba?

"Shontelle, I owe you this," he said softly. "You owe it to me, as well."

She stared at the steadily burning purpose in his eyes. "How do you work that out?" she challenged.

"You let them picture me falsely. Because they got away with it, they will go on picturing me falsely to others whenever it suits their purpose. That must be stopped, and the most effective way of stopping it is for you to bear witness for me in a court where it will count, in front of people who count to them. Together we can throw their game back in their faces."

She shivered at the ruthless intent behind his words. "As you did with me last night, Luis?" she said, reminding him of that wretched outcome.

"No. That was not justice. It was the vengeance of a man whose love had been robbed of all value. And it will always haunt me as a shameful act on my part. But there is no shame in seeking justice, Shontelle. Only shame in not pursuing it."

He was right in a way. It was wrong to let Elvira

Rosa Martinez and Claudia Gallardo get away scot-free with what they'd done. Justice…it gave a kind of closure to a crime. And it had been a crime…the premeditated murder of love.

It wouldn't take much, she argued to herself. Just one more night. For his pride. For her pride. But how could she carry it off? "I don't have anything suitable to wear, Luis. They'd all look down their noses at me and think you mad for bringing me into their midst."

"I'll provide you with appropriate clothes. I'll have a selection delivered to my apartment. With the finest accessories." He flashed a wicked smile that jiggled her heart. "Believe me, you will not be underdressed for this occasion."

Wealth, Shontelle sternly reminded herself, was one of the divisive factors she could not overlook. Obscene wealth. Luis could probably order anything to appear at the snap of his fingers. Or a telephone call. Though there were some things one couldn't buy… like love and trust and happiness.

"Is it worth it to you, Luis?" she asked. "Even if we manage to get to Santa Cruz by seven o'clock, it's then a three hour flight to Buenos Aires. Add on the hour time difference, plus time to dress ourselves appropriately. I doubt we could make it to the reception before midnight."

"Yes, it's worth it," he asserted strongly. "And I consider midnight perfect timing. Everyone will be there by then and no one would have left. It would be seen as rude to leave such an elite gathering before

3:00 a.m.'' Another flash of wickedness. "We shall make quite an entrance, you and I.''

He relished the idea. And suddenly Shontelle did, too. Why not? "You intend to turn the pumpkin into a princess at the stroke of midnight?'' she half mocked.

"You were never a pumpkin,'' he shot back at her, anger flaring from his eyes. "Do not ever regard yourself in such a demeaning light. You are...'' His lips compressed, shutting off the line of thought he'd been about to give voice to. He shook his head in an anguished roll. "It is wrong to hate one's mother. But I do hate much of what's she's done.''

The torment so clearly expressed moved Shontelle more than anything else he'd said. She thought of her own mother who was always there for her, ready to give any help or comfort, always looking to answer her needs without ever forcing anything. For all the wealth at his disposal, it had not been an easy life for Luis, always feeling the load of responsibility he'd inherited through his older brother's death.

She remembered all the things he'd confided to her when they'd been most intimate. He had never openly criticised his mother for the way she had ordered his life so he could take Eduardo's place, but she had sensed he sometimes felt trapped in a role that had been thrust upon him. Once he had said he envied Alan's freedom to choose his own path.

"I have to break the chains that have bound me for so long,'' he muttered. Then his hand reached across and took hers, interlacing their fingers in a tight, forceful grip that throbbed with intense feeling. "Be my partner tonight, Shontelle. I will see that you catch your flight home to Australia tomorrow. But tonight is ours...one final stand together...for justice."

"Yes," she agreed, barely aware of giving her consent.

She was overwhelmingly aware of the physical link he had just forged. Except somehow it was more than physical. It was like a current flowing from him and flooding every cell of her body. She stared down at their hands, not understanding, only knowing she ached with a terrible need to stay joined to him.

She forgot the other factors.

Suddenly they were meaningless.

If only Luis would hold on to her, she would stand with him to the end of time.

CHAPTER THIRTEEN

"THE red," Luis said decisively.

"Are you sure?" Shontelle asked, her gaze clinging to the safer, black lace creation.

She still couldn't quite believe the array of beautiful designer clothes and accessories laid out for her to choose from in the main bedroom of Luis' apartment. It was difficult enough, coping with being hit by the familiarity of a room they had shared so intimately. Besides which, the prospect of returning to the Martinez mansion had her nerves in a jangling mess, despite having the promised security of Luis' arm to support her. She was afraid of looking wrong.

"Melding into the crowd is not what tonight is about, Shontelle," Luis dryly reminded her.

Not the black then. "The gold one is very elegant," she pointed out.

"Wear the red." No doubt, no reservation in his voice.

"Luis, it hardly has any back to it," she protested worriedly. The gown dipped right down to waist level, apparently supported by a silver Y-strap running down her spine and two shoestring red straps that joined it to hold the bodice firmly across her breasts.

"You have a beautiful back."

The soft, thick words raised goose bumps all over her skin. Her heart thumped erratically. She knew she could still arouse desire in him. Last night had proved that. Even when he'd hated her the sexual chemistry hadn't waned. But tonight wasn't about answering those needs, was it? He'd given no indication of it.

"That doesn't mean I should bare it," she said, keeping her gaze fixed firmly on the dress, as though studying its potential to embarrass her.

Her mind was jagging off in wild directions. This togetherness project was bound to push them into more intimacy as the night went on…holding, dancing, continual linking with each other. What if it led back to this bed? What if they ended up making love? Would he ask her to stay with him…or would he stick to his promise to have her at the airport tomorrow in good time to join Alan and the tour group for their flight home?

"Your hair will veil most of it," he said, his voice even more furred with sensual overtones.

"I thought I'd put it up. It's more sophisticated," she almost gabbled in helpless agitation.

"No. Wear it loose. And wear the red, Shontelle." She heard his breath hiss out on a long sigh. "I will leave you to dress. The bathroom is free for your use."

His footsteps moved to the spare bedroom. Its door clicked shut. He was giving her complete privacy, removing any sense of lurking intimacy she might feel. And did feel. One night…for justice, he'd said. Did she dare reach for more? Was *more* possible?

Dear God! Hadn't she hoped the same last night? She'd be totally mad to lay herself on the line again. Just get on with what's been planned, she savagely berated herself, and grabbed the make-up that had been supplied to complement the red dress. The bathroom was free and there was no time to waste.

Nevertheless, as she took a quick shower and set about adding glamour to her face, she couldn't stop her mind from wandering over Luis' manner to her since she had agreed to his plan. Apart from the one strong hand grip, he hadn't touched her, nor said anything suggestive of a sexual interest or any interest in her beyond tonight.

Unfinished business, he'd told Alan when he'd asked they be dropped at the Santa Cruz airport before the tour group was driven on to their hotel. Alan had simply asked her, "Is this your choice, Shontelle?" and when she'd answered, "Yes," he'd set the scene for her and Luis' departure, explaining to the group that Luis had supplied them with the bus as a special favour to the Amigos Tours Company and they were returning the favour in helping him to make an important business connection on time. Shontelle's accompanying him to Buenos Aires on a private flight would place her there to deal with any problems arising tomorrow.

No one had protested.

On their arrival at the airport, it had been all business. The moment the bus pulled up, a man from the Martinez company had been on the spot to escort them to the company plane. He'd handed Luis an attaché case which Shontelle had deduced contained important company documents, then taken charge of her luggage. The tour group gave them a rousing farewell, happy that their journey was almost over, Alan wished them well, and their escort whisked them away.

There was no delay in taking off. Once safely in the air, they were served dinner, after which Luis had urged her to get some rest and moved to another part of the plane, presumably to work on the papers in the attaché case. She'd actually slept for most of the flight, the toll of a long day's travelling following a wretched night of distress finally wearing out her too active mind. Luis woke her as they were about to land, awakening her senses, too, as she breathed in the cologne he'd splashed onto his freshly shaven face.

His shaving on the flight had probably been done to leave his bathroom free for her, she thought now, but right then, in her drowsy state, she'd almost reached up and touched his face, only just halting the movement and redirecting her hand to scrape an errant strand of hair off her own face. But the impulse had rattled her. She shouldn't still want him so... wantonly. She knew it was foolish.

The subsequent drive from the airport to this apartment had been fraught with tension on her part. They didn't talk. It was a company car with a chauffeur doing the driving. The silver-grey Mercedes with its plush interior was clearly executive class. The power of wealth was being demonstrated in full, ever since she'd agreed to standing with Luis tonight.

A final stand...

Final!

She had to get that through her head.

Tonight was the end, no chance at all of a new beginning.

Having emphasised her eyes with subtle earth tones and put a glow on her skin with the clever cosmetics designed for that purpose, Shontelle outlined her mouth with the red pencil provided and filled in the curves with a vivid scarlet lipstick, the perfect match for the dress Luis had insisted upon.

The thought occurred to her she'd certainly be a scarlet woman tonight to at least two people. Or a flaming sword, cutting their lies down and laying them waste. Which was what those wicked lies deserved, defaming Luis and deceiving her with such devastating results.

Justice...

Satisfied she'd at least done justice to her face, Shontelle put the lipstick down, unbraided her hair, and brushed it into a cloud of rippling waves. The plait had crinkled it and there was no time to wash and dry it into a straight fall, but it was still clean and shiny from last night's washing. Luis had always preferred it loose. She hoped it didn't look too untamed and casual to other eyes.

Wrapped in a towel, she collected her things and dashed back to the bedroom. Luis was nowhere in view. She hurried through the nervous business of dressing herself to the standard expected of a guest at a Martinez grand reception.

The red gown was spectacular. The fabric was soft and slinky and woven through with silver thread, creating a kind of oriental design of meandering vines and leaves that shimmered exotically on the scarlet background. It clung to every curve of her body, only flaring slightly from the knees so she could walk comfortably.

The silver shoulder straps extended down the outside curve of her breasts and joined underneath them, creating a bra effect with the fabric stretched above and between them. Shontelle worried over the cleavage on display until she added the fine filigree silver chains and necklaces that cascaded from her throat, filling in the expanse of bare flesh and adding that indefinable sense of class to sexiness.

Beautiful silver strappy high heels and an elegant little silver handbag gave the perfect touches of completion. Shontelle couldn't help staring at her reflection in the mirror, amazed by the transformation that could be wrought, given no expense spared for anything. Fine feathers certainly made fine birds. Even to herself she looked stunning. Which gave her a much-needed boost in confidence.

She quickly put the scarlet lipstick, a couple of tissues and some emergency money into the tiny evening bag. The bedside clock read 11:43. Luis' estimate of a midnight arrival at the reception was going to be very close, assuming he was also ready to leave now. Time to find out, she told herself, taking a deep breath and hoping the flutters in her stomach didn't get any worse.

He was waiting for her, just standing in the middle of the living room, nursing a drink in one hand. The sheer impact of him, dressed in formal evening clothes, brought Shontelle to a halt. His black dinner suit had the expensive sheen of silk, and its black satin lapels and matching bow tie added a sensual touch against the crisp whiteness of his finely pintucked shirt. He looked utterly superb and so handsome, Shontelle could hardly breathe, let alone walk.

The perfect man, she thought—tall, dark, handsome and loaded with a brooding, male animal appeal that was all the more enticing for being encased in the clothes of sophisticated civilisation. Her heart was going haywire, frantically signalling that *he* was the man for her, and if she let him go, she would be losing the mate of her life. But how could she make it right between them? How?

"The sun and the moon and the stars..."

The soft murmur from Luis seemed to feather down her spine. His eyes glowed the kind of warmth she'd all but forgotten, stirring memories of beautiful times together, times of tenderness and deep, inexpressible joy. Hope leapt into her mind and danced through her veins. Then his thick lashes lowered, shadowing the look that belonged to an idyll of blissful togetherness, and his mouth curved into an ironic little smile.

"You'll outshine them all tonight. As you should. Though I would have been proud to present you whatever you wore, Shontelle. I don't suppose you'll believe that, but it's true."

"I want to do you proud, Luis," she answered, feeling he was making light of the power of first impressions. Not that he'd care...if tonight was the end. First impressions would only be important to him if she were to stay in his social circle. But just this once, Shontelle wanted to feel acceptable in his world, and see acceptance in others' eyes. It was important to her that she didn't fail this test.

His brows drew together in a quick frown. "If you feel...not right..." He gestured an apologetic appeal. "I should not have pressed you to wear anything you prefer not to."

"No. I like the red on me," she quickly assured him.

His concern broke into a grin of sheer, wicked pleasure. "Good! It is absolutely perfect for you in my eyes. I shall enjoy being the envy of every man at the reception."

He set his glass down on a table as he moved to open the door with a flourish, his grin still alight with devilish anticipation. "Come, Cinderella. It is time to go to the ball."

A nervous laugh bubbled out of her throat as she forced her legs to move. Elvira Rosa Martinez wasn't exactly the wicked stepmother and Claudia Gallardo couldn't be described as an ugly stepsister, but Shontelle couldn't help hoping they'd get the shock of their lives when they recognised who had the Prince's arm tonight.

The silver Mercedes was waiting for them. The chauffeur saw Shontelle settled on one side of the back seat while Luis rounded the car and took the other side. They were closed in together for the final act.

Five more minutes and the players would be on stage, Shontelle thought, wondering just how many people would be shocked by her appearance with Luis Angel Martinez, the heir to a fortune, who was undoubtedly expected to be paying court to the heiress of a fortune. A worrisome thought struck her and she turned sharply to Luis as the car moved off.

"What about the Gallardo family? Will this make bad business between you?"

"I don't care, Shontelle. What will be, will be," he said quietly, firmly.

Reckless?

She studied him for a moment, but his expression was difficult to read in the shadows of the night. He sat back, apparently perfectly relaxed, yet she could feel the harnessing of power and purpose in him, the determination to sweep all before him, to stamp his own will on everything that happened.

"Don't fear anything on my account, Shontelle," he said softly. "Whatever the consequences of tonight, I would rather be known as my own man than have others think they own me."

"It's strange to me...this Martinez side of you... the public position you hold in Argentina. You never really showed it to me."

"I preferred you to know the private person."

"I don't think you can separate yourself out like that, Luis."

"It was wrong," he agreed. "You have made me see that very clearly, Shontelle. For which I am deeply grateful. A man cannot live another's life. He must be true to himself."

Shontelle suddenly perceived tonight wasn't so much about justice to Luis. It was about freedom. Which made it a far more momentous occasion than she had realised. He was seeing this as a major turning point in his life...and *she* had done this?

A shiver ran down her spine.

No, she argued frantically. I'm only the catalyst. He wasn't happy. He probably hadn't been happy for many, many years. Even in his mind, his love affair with her had been time stolen from a life he found oppressive, time for himself. Which was probably why he'd been so frustrated and embittered when she'd ended it.

Had he ever really loved her? Or had she represented something he'd needed...a rebellion against the structure he'd been born into...an outlet for feelings he couldn't normally express…a refuge from pressures that seemed ultimately inescapable?

There were so many layers to him she didn't know. She had loved him instinctively. Still did. Impulsively she reached over and lightly squeezed his arm. "I'm with you tonight, Luis. Whatever you want to achieve, I'm on your side."

Before she could withdraw her hand he caught it, trapped it, transmitting a burst of energy that zinged up her arm and raced through her whole nervous system. "Is that a promise, Shontelle?" he asked, and even in the darkness his eyes blazed with an intensity that shot quivers through her heart.

"Yes," she whispered.

"Then the sun and the moon and the stars shine on me tonight," he said, and laughed, tilting his head back and giving vent to a peal of joyous, devil-may-care laughter.

Even as Shontelle stared at him in startled wonder, he lifted her hand to his lips and pressed a warm kiss across her knuckles. His eyes sobered, but a winsome smile lingered on his mouth as he said, "Thank you. Though I will not hold you to such an all-encompassing promise, Shontelle. I would not want you to rue it. You are free to choose whatever is right for you."

Free…her heart sank, taking with it the foolish hopes that had persisted in fluttering, despite a strong dose of common sense. He did not want her to tie herself to him. This partnership was mutual in so far as they had a common purpose in seeking justice, but there the mutuality ended. He could not have spelled the position out more clearly.

The car slowed, turned, and the huge black iron gates that guarded the Martinez mansion caught her eye.

They were here!

The impressive Graeco-Roman edifice with its massive columns and elaborate cornices was stage-lit from the gardens on either side of the driveway. Music drifted from the opened doors to the second-story balconies which led off the ballroom. The grand reception was clearly in full swing.

The Mercedes stopped at the flight of steps which was framed by a portico that would have done a temple proud. It was a temple, Shontelle thought with painful irony, a temple to all Elvira Rosa Martinez held dear. The question tonight was...which did she hold more dear, her son or his heritage? The choice was almost upon her.

Luis released her hand to alight from the car, quickly skirting it to lend his arm to Shontelle's emergence on the other side. The chauffeur held her door open. She gathered her skirt up carefully to avoid any problem with it as she stepped out.

Red...the colour of danger.

Too late to retreat now.

She'd given her word.

Luis took her hand again, and as she straightened up beside him he tucked her arm around his in a pro-

prietary gesture that proclaimed their public togetherness.

"Ready?" he asked, his eyes gleaming some deep,
personal satisfaction.

"Yes," she answered, resolved on facing the people who had brought her—brought both Luis and
her—to this final act.

Arm in arm, they moved up the steps.

And somewhere in the distance, a clock tolled midnight.

CHAPTER FOURTEEN

"SEÑOR MARTINEZ!" The surprise on the elderly manservant's face was echoed in his voice as he ushered them into the foyer. "It was not expected..." He looked in confusion at Shontelle, who was undoubtedly even more unexpected.

"I had some luck getting out of La Paz," Luis explained.

"Your mother will be..." He choked on whatever word he might ordinarily have used—pleased, delighted, ecstatic—staring at Shontelle in a kind of dazed horror.

"May I introduce my companion, Miss Shontelle Wright. Shontelle, this is..."

"Carlos," she broke in. "We've met before." She smiled at the elderly retainer whose skin had gone quite sallow. "You served me with lunch here, two years ago, though you may not remember me."

"Sí, Miss Wright," he answered faintly, then swallowed hard. "I shall go and announce your arrival."

Luis reached out and stayed the man before he could move. "Let's pretend I let myself in, Carlos. I wish to surprise my mother."

"But, *Señor*..."

Steely authority instantly emerged. "I'd advise you

to look the other way, Carlos. Do I make myself clear?''

''Sí, señor.''

He backed off and Luis swept Shontelle onto the grand staircase which led to the long gallery bordering the ballroom; the gallery of gold-framed portraits and priceless objets d'art that had so overwhelmed her on her last visit here.

They mounted the stairs, meeting no resistance from other household staff. The music was louder now, an orchestra of master tango musicians playing traditional *porteno* arrangements on violins and the unique Argentinian version of squeeze-boxes, *bandoneons.*

''Remember dancing the tango with me?'' Luis murmured.

She glanced at him, flushing at the memories he'd evoked; the wildly erotic movements they'd practised in private, teasing each other with a pretence of discipline and control, throwing themselves into the beat of the music for the sheer dramatic fun of it...and always ending up making passionate love to each other.

His eyes caught hers, and she saw he was thinking of those times, too. ''It was good,'' she answered huskily, her pulse beat speeding up at the simmering look he returned.

''Poetry and fire...it is a dance of the soul, yes?''

She nodded, unsure what he wanted from her. Historically, the tango had evolved from a *darkness* of soul, more an expression of tragic pain than any-thing else...men without women, dancing alone, working off their despair with life. Was Luis feeling some parallel with that history now?

"Will you dance it with me tonight?" he asked.

A last tango? Her legs quivered at the prospect. To her the dance was associated with very raw, uninhibited desire. Was it sensible to tempt fate when there was no future in it? An unaccountable surge of recklessness overrode wisdom.

"If you think it's appropriate," she said.

"I find poetry and fire particularly appropriate in this instance."

Dante's *Inferno* slipped into Shontelle's mind. Were the devils in hell dancing tonight? Luis seemed intent on using every bit of firepower to blow his mother's ambitions for him apart. *I'm his torch,* she thought, and wondered if there'd be anything other than ashes left over when all the burning had been done.

He'd mockingly named this place a mausoleum, she recalled, as they stepped past the marble arch that marked the entrance to the gallery. It might contain treasures of the dead but Shontelle was made instantly aware of very alive people occupying it. Groups of guests were viewing items of interest or just chatting amongst themselves, taking a break from the ballroom.

The late appearance of Luis Angel Martinez with an unknown woman in tow was swiftly noticed. Conversation stopped. Heads craned. Shontelle was acutely sensitive to the wave of shock rolling down the entire showroom, and it was her presence causing it, or rather her being partnered by Luis. Eyes busily assessed her appearance. Whispers started. Shontelle imagined people hastily asking... *Who is she? What does this mean?*

One man broke away from his circle of companions and hurried towards them. Shontelle's heart did a little skip as she recognised him as Luis' younger brother, Patricio. He looked bewildered, unable to believe his eyes, yet driven to ascertain what the situation was.

"*¡Dios!* This is some entrance, Luis!" he muttered, deliberately blocking their way.

His physique was shorter and leaner than his older brother's but there was a tensile strength about him that made him a formidable opponent if he wished to be. His moustache gave his handsome face a rather dashing, playboy air, which was deceptive. Shontelle knew him to be an exacting and shrewd businessman who managed the Martinez agricultural interests with a very astute reading of marketability. He occasionally showed off his brilliant horsemanship to tour groups who visited the main ranch outside Buenos Aires, but Alan had told her that was the only playing Luis' brother indulged in.

"Move aside, Patricio," Luis commanded in an equally low voice.

"You're supposed to be in La Paz," came the confused protest.

"Get out of my way," Luis warned. "And please give Shontelle the courtesy of a greeting. You have met Alan's sister."

"Shontelle?" He did a double take, staring at her with suddenly enlightened eyes. "I did not recognise you. And this..." His long Spanish nose lifted haughtily as he glared back at Luis. "...This I do not understand."

"You don't have to," Luis tersely informed him.

"You yourself declared any member of the Wright family persona non grata," Patricio retorted fiercely.

"The betrayal of trust was not theirs. I did them an injustice I am bound to correct."

"There's a time and place for everything, Luis. This isn't it," Patricio argued.

"There is none better in my opinion."

"Are you mad? The Gallardo family is here in full force. You cannot flaunt another woman in Claudia's face."

"Oh, yes I can."

The venom in Luis' voice jolted Patricio. He turned a beetling frown on Shontelle. "I mean no offence to you, Shontelle, but this is a situation of some delicacy. My mother intends to announce..."

"She will not," Luis cut in. "I informed her it was not possible when I called about the situation in La Paz. I told her I would select a time of my own choosing."

Patricio shook his head. "Your supposed absence was not going to stop it, Luis. You gave your tacit approval before you left for La Paz. When the orchestra finishes their performance…''

"So she would force my hand…even to this," Luis grated. His face was thunderous as he shot out an arm to hold Patricio at a distance while he steered Shontelle around him with such alacrity, she almost tripped trying to keep up.

Patricio fell into step beside him, urgently pleading. "Luis, this is tantamount to committing harakiri in public."

"She leaves me no choice."

"Let me take care of Shontelle. You can ride this through and…"

"No." Luis instantly secured Shontelle's hold on his arm by clamping his free hand over hers, deliberately emphasising their togetherness as he moved relentlessly forward. "There will be no more riding anything through at my mother's will," he seethed at his brother.

"Luis, what is this about?" Shontelle pleaded, agitated by the turbulent currents in the conversation. "You said it was a glittering occasion but if it has some important meaning…"

"His engagement to Claudia Gallardo is about to be announced," Patricio shot at her.

"What?" she cried in horror.

"No!" Luis denied vehemently. "It will not happen. I will not allow it to happen."

Shontelle's feet faltered as she was hit by the enormity of what he had kept from her. "But you knew…

Oh, my God! You brought me here, knowing…and last night…''

He halted to face her, his eyes blazing into hers. ''*I* have not given Claudia a commitment, Shontelle.''

''You let them think it was on the cards,'' Patricio sliced in, moving to close them into a private little circle.

''The cards got reshuffled today and they will never be the same again,'' Luis fired at his brother. ''I am reclaiming my life. Wear Eduardo's shoes yourself if all this means so much to you. They probably fit you a lot better than they do me.''

Patricio recoiled a step, his face reflecting intense inner turmoil. ''I don't want it, Luis.''

''Then don't shovel it on me.''

''Luis…this is wrong…you didn't tell me how it was,'' Shontelle cried, plucking at the hand holding hers, hating the feeling of being used.

''Did Claudia care for you? Did my mother let us be?'' he flashed at her with such violent feeling, it shook Shontelle from her bid to detach herself from him. ''You said you would stand by me,'' he went on passionately. ''Can I count on no one?''

His eyes burned with a terrible need that sucked relentlessly on Shontelle's heart, draining it of resistance to what he was asking of her. She was part of the pattern of deceit that had riddled his life and that guilt still remained, twisting inside her. Yet two wrongs didn't make a right and he had let her believe—led her to believe—there was no relationship with Claudia worth talking about.

"You repeat your own error in holding things from me, Luis," she reminded him, unwilling to let his fault pass without comment.

"The issue of justice was the same," he insisted.

Was it? Somehow the imminent engagement muddied everything. The thought of him courting Claudia, kissing her... "Have you made love to her?" she asked, riven by the stark memory of what he'd done last night with no love at all.

"*¡Cristo!*" Patricio expostulated. "She has no right..."

"*¡Silencio!* It is you who has no right!" Luis snapped, then swung his gaze back to Shontelle, urgently begging belief. "I was never even tempted to make love to her." His look of repugnance reinforced his claim. "There was absolutely no intimacy between me and Claudia Gallardo."

"Then how could this engagement come about?" she cried in torment.

"It was a matter of indifference to me whom I married. Claudia pursued it. My mother pushed it. *You* had left me to them."

Her fault? Was this justice or vengeance? A last tango with him...dark, dark angel.

"Luis, the music has stopped," Patricio warned.

"Shontelle...am I alone?" he pressed, still searing her soul with his eyes.

The tug was stronger than ever, despite the dreadful

confusion swirling around it. She gave up the fight to understand. If it meant so much to him—that she stand by him now—using her to gain his freedom— then why not do it? At least it would expunge her guilt over how she'd scarred his life.

"No," she whispered. "I'm with you."

He released a long shuddering breath and quickly acted on her consent, walking them both on. She could hear people gathering behind them, following them, drawn by the promise of scandal. The scarlet woman indeed, Shontelle thought, beginning to feel quite light-headed.

As they rounded the corner of the gallery to the shorter section which opened into the ballroom, Patricio slipped behind Luis and stepped up beside Shontelle so she was flanked by both men. The three of them walking abreast drew attention from the people they were approaching. More stares. Buzzing speculation.

"Better peel off, Patricio," Luis advised.

"No."

"This is my fight."

"I don't know what the hell is behind this, Luis, but if you're vacating Eduardo's shoes, she's not going to put me into them. I'll stand with you."

"This a highly personal affair, Patricio."

"Better we present a united front."

"A bit late for that, given your attempt to stop me."

"Not too late for the main event."

Stubborn resolve from Patricio, reckless resolve from Luis. Between them, Shontelle felt carried along towards some kind of Armageddon, a clash of power that promised the end of an era of domination. And here she was, dressed like a princess to be a pawn in the battle. No, not a pawn, she decided. A symbol. A weapon. A flaming sword for truth and justice.

She smiled at that thought...definitely light-headed. The words of the song—*Don't Cry For Me, Argentina*—flitted through her mind as they entered the ballroom. The aristocracy was all around her now, very distinguished-looking men, women lavishly bejewelled. She was being inspected by them. Shontelle held her head high—Cinderella at the ball, escorted by the Martinez princes.

Then from the other end of the ballroom, a voice rang out over a microphone, a voice Shontelle instantly recognised as belonging to the woman reputed to be the wealthiest and most powerful woman in Argentina.

"My friends...thank you for coming this evening. It gives me much pleasure to see you all here, to join with me in celebrating a very special event. Unfortunately, my son, Luis, has been trapped in La Paz, due to..."

"No, *Madre*... Luis has come," Patricio called out.

It was as though he had pointed a staff like Moses. The sea of people in front of them parted, fell back, and a clear path opened up down the length of the dance floor to the dais where Elvira Rosa Martinez stood like an all-powerful pharaoh in command of her world.

She looked magnificent, dressed in shimmering royal blue, with a fabulous collar of gold around her throat, gold falling from her ears and circling her wrists. The hand holding the microphone sparkled with ornate rings. But her handsome face lost its winning smile as she realised what was facing her.

Not Luis alone.

Not Luis with his younger brother.

Not Luis, miraculously arriving in time to pledge himself to the woman his mother had ordained he marry.

On his arm was another woman, possessively secured there by a hand that proclaimed her his in no uncertain terms.

Shontelle had no idea if Elvira recognised her but the message being telegraphed was unmistakable, to everyone looking on. This was a parade of proud defiance of what anyone thought. This was a statement of arrogant independence. The gauntlet had been thrown in front of every high-ranking person in the country and there was no turning back from it.

CHAPTER FIFTEEN

A SILENCE fell, and it seemed to Shontelle there was a freezing of time in the Martinez mansion. The huge gilt-framed mirrors in the ballroom reflected a scene that had stopped moving. Overhead the many-tiered chandeliers were brilliantly alight, glowing with a life of their own. Below them, she and Luis and Patricio walked in unison, a pace measured by dignity...no haste...no falter.

The sound of their footsteps on the parquet floor was eerie...isolated...echoing in a weird emptiness. Luis and Patricio were stepping into an unknown future, Shontelle thought, and risking all they'd had in the past for it. Was it worth it to them? Was it? She didn't know what it was like to be shackled by a heritage such as theirs. Impossible for her to weigh the prizes and penalties of great wealth.

Elvira...staring at them, her expression oddly glazed.

Open rebellion facing her.

Would she act to stop it?

Did she sense there was no stopping it?

Shontelle's nerves prickled as Elvira's gaze focused on her, her eyes suddenly sharp with recognition. Yes, she thought fiercely. Look at me. Look at your victim of yesteryear and feel the wheel turning. It's right that it should.

Elvira's head turned slightly, her gaze shooting to a group of people gathered to the right of the stage. And there was Claudia Gallardo, presumably surrounded by her family. Claudia, dressed in pure virginal white, a bridal beacon, masking the calculating mind that had sacrificed integrity in her ruthless push to an altar of greed. Claudia, staring at them in disbelief, not receiving whatever mental message her co-conspirator had tried to send.

Frustrated and aware of the electric curiosity aroused, Luis' mother sought to distract, as well as soothe the escalating tension, using the microphone to draw attention back to her. "Well, this is a wonderful surprise! It appears nothing—not even a revolution in Bolivia—could keep Luis from joining us tonight. Please forgive a short delay while I welcome him home."

She turned and gestured to the violinists to play. They quickly struck up a tune. Elvira set the microphone on its stand and moved regally to the left-hand side of the stage, away from the Gallardo family, a blatant directive to Luis to accommodate her wish to have a private word with him before he committed himself to what she undoubtedly saw as ultimate folly.

Luis did not oblige her.

Without hesitation, he aimed the three of them straight towards the Gallardo family. Patricio needed no signal. He adjusted his step to keep the united front. A march into the face of enemy lines, Shontelle thought, seeing a bristling start to run through the family who had expected to seal an important liaison this night.

Did they know what had been done in pursuit of it? The Gallardo men were older than Luis and Patricio. Much older. Had they viewed Luis Angel Martinez as a bunny to be taken for what he was worth?

Well, meet the rabbit in the hat, Shontelle thought with wild irreverence for their fortune-melding. She locked her eyes onto the dark, dazed gaze of the heiress who'd cut Shontelle's faith in Luis' love into irredeemable fragments, and all her grief boiled up into a blistering challenge.

How do you like it, Claudia, being faced with a partnership you thought you'd destroyed? Being faced with the woman you lied to? Seeing the future you'd hoped for dashed into dust?

The answer was not long in coming.

There was a sudden snap of recognition…the realisation of what Shontelle's appearance with Luis had to mean…then fury…sheer black fury. No broken heart in those eyes as they slashed down Shontelle's dressed-to-kill gown and whipped up to the man she'd almost won with the connivance of his mother. The fury switched to a haughty contempt. No way was Claudia Gallardo going to be bowed in defeat.

"I see you've taken up with your foreign trash

again, Luis,'' she attacked first, just as they halted directly in front of her.

Shontelle's hackles rose. It was difficult to treat such an insult with disdain, but she did her best to project unassailable confidence in her right to be at Luis' side. Apart from which, this was his fight. He proceeded to answer his erstwhile fiancée with icy control.

''I leave it to you to explain to your family why I do what I do now, Claudia. And may I suggest you curb your malicious spite. It will not serve you well.''

''Explain to *me!*'' the elderly man beside Claudia demanded brusquely. ''You serve us with a public humiliation. It is not to be forgiven, Luis.''

''Esteban, your daughter and my mother contrived to destroy the most precious thing in my life. Do not speak of forgiveness to me. I will see justice done first.''

For a moment, Shontelle's heart swelled painfully. Hearing Luis call the love they'd shared *the most precious thing in his life* made the loss all the harder to bear.

''What justice?'' the old man spluttered. ''Patricio...'' he appealed, ''...is this an act of honour?''

''You cannot divide me from my brother, Esteban,'' came the hard warning. ''We will have truth tonight and there is no dishonour in truth.''

''We had an understanding!'' Esteban protested fiercely.

''Built on deception,'' Luis accused.

"You can prove this?"

"Ask your daughter," Luis repeated with steely force. Then with a harsh edge of suspicion, he added, "If you don't already know of the lies she spun to engage me with your family."

The Gallardo patriarch flushed in anger. "To what are you referring?"

"Clean your own house, Esteban…as I now clean mine."

Luis inclined his head slightly, a token respect to the old man, then wheeled their small procession towards the other side of the stage where his mother was waiting.

"Foreign trash," Claudia sniped again.

"Hold your tongue, girl, and put your best face forward," Esteban commanded tersely. "You will not shame me in this company."

Luis Angel Martinez was no bunny and would never be taken by any of these people as anything but a man to be reckoned with, Shontelle thought with intense pride. She savagely wished she had given him the chance to stand up for her two years ago. She knew now, beyond a shadow of a doubt, he would have done it, would have challenged his mother then and there and fought to keep what was *precious* to him.

Tears pricked her eyes. She'd been so stupidly gullible. Yet looking at the woman—Luis' formidable mother—who had played her hand with such subtle but devastating force, Shontelle knew she'd had no defences against such cleverly harnessed power. She had needed a champion, such as Luis had shown himself to be tonight.

Stand by me...

Was he drawing strength from her support?

She willed back the moisture threatening to film her eyes. People were watching. Elvira Rosa Martinez was watching. To cover the snub by Luis, she had moved on to the group of people closest to the other side of the stage, smiling, chatting, as though there was nothing amiss—

"The sister of a very enterprising tour operator. An old friend of Luis'," Shontelle imagined her explaining. "They must have been in La Paz, too. They've obviously managed to get out together. Heaven knows how..."

But Elvira needed space to confront the only truth that mattered to her. She excused herself to meet her sons, and there could be no misreading the battle light in her eyes. The queen was not amused at having her act upstaged and sabotaged.

Shontelle braced herself. Elvira would certainly consider her the weak spot, the most vulnerable to attack. It was vitally important to show no weakness whatsoever. Luis was counting on her to play her part through. If this was a courtroom, the jury was all around her, judging her performance. She had to prove worthy of being championed by both the Martinez men.

"Could you not have faced me first, Luis?" she lashed at him in fury.

"You did not face me at all two years ago, Mother," he retorted.

"It was for your own good," she retaliated. "Which, if you had any sense, you would recognise."

"And for my good, you would wed me to a cold, lying bitch! Step aside, Mother."

"No. I will not let you throw all I've worked for away."

"Your needs are not mine. Accept me for the man I am or *you* throw it away. Who else have you got, Mother?"

The challenge could not be borne. She fixed a commanding gaze on her younger son. "Patricio..."

"No." His rejection was sharp and immediate. Then with quiet and resolute force, Patricio stated, "I will not carry the load you demanded of Luis. I am content with what I am."

Thwarted, she raked Shontelle with bitter scorn. "This woman...how can she be worth bringing us down?"

"Down from what?" Luis mocked. "The prison you have made for me out of Eduardo's death?"

She flinched. "How dare you..."

"How dare you abrogate my rights to my own life?" His voice vibrated with outrage.

Elvira's chin lifted in arrogant pride. "She is not even Argentinian."

Foreign trash...

"She is the woman I love, Mother."

Love? Shontelle's heart stopped. Had she heard right? Did Luis mean it or...

"You could try to remember how that feels," he went on with hard, driving passion. "The intense joy of it, Mother. The sheer exhilarating splendour of it. Look into the cold little coffin you call your heart and dredge out what you felt for my father. Or even more, for Eduardo."

"Stop this!" Her face was drained of colour.

"Just once. Do it! I'm your son, too. As is Patricio."

"It's because you are, I've done what I've done to protect you," she argued.

"We are men. We do not need or want your protection."

"Eduardo would not have died..."

"Eduardo is gone. And I shall lead my own life...with or without you. Your choice, Mother."

"Luis, you can't..."

"Watch me! Shontelle?"

The call of her name and the slight tug on her arm jolted Shontelle out of her absorption in the deep conflict between mother and son. She looked up at Luis, unsure what had been said in truth or for telling effect.

"It is your turn now," he said, his eyes burning with a purpose she didn't comprehend.

Did he mean her turn to say something to his mother? Surely he realised it was irrelevant.

"Patricio…" He glanced over her head at his brother. "…The stage is mine."

"We will stand by and watch," he replied. "Won't we, *Madre?*"

Shontelle didn't see or hear a response from Elvira. Luis swept her around his mother, heading for the steps at the side of the stage. "What do you plan to do?" she whispered urgently.

Surely there was nothing left to be achieved. The announcement his mother was to have made had been stopped and rendered impossible. Was Luis going to make some kind of public relations speech to cover the breech?

He bent his head closer to hers. "Shontelle, you are free to choose as you wish." His voice was low, intense, his eyes scouring hers. "Have I done enough?" he muttered, seemingly to himself.

His words made no sense to her. "You've set everything as right as you can," she assured him.

"No. I stripped you down to nothing last night. I know it is something you will never forget. But, Shontelle, I offer you now the chance to do the same to me. You can reject all I am in front of everyone, and I will not blame you for it. It is your just due."

"Luis…" He was frightening her. "I don't want this…this atonement."

"Then accept my gift for the spirit in which it is given."

"What gift?"

"You will see…and I hope…understand."

Already he was drawing her up the steps to the stage. Bewildered and apprehensive, Shontelle could barely respond to the smile he flashed at her as he unhooked their arms and caught her hand. He signalled to the violinists to stop playing, which they very promptly did.

The sudden cessation of music was like a clarion call to the crowd, galvanising attention on the stage which had been vacated by Elvira Rosa Martinez and now starred her son, Luis Angel, and the woman in red.

The general hush was loaded with fascinated anticipation. The Gallardo family had not walked out. Elvira Rosa Martinez stood with her younger son, Patricio, apparently at ease with this curious development. An announcement had been promised. A celebration was supposed to ensue. When Luis took hold of the microphone, one could have heard a pin drop in the ballroom.

Shontelle found herself holding her breath and forced herself to relax. As far as she was concerned, justice had been carried out. Whatever Luis did now was for himself. She had no further axe to grind.

Only his declaration of loving her remained a private torment. She wished it was true. But his reminder of last night's wretched travesty of intimacy...how could that equate with love?

He squeezed her hand, transmitting a bolt of tingling warmth, distracting her from her feverish thoughts.

She looked at him, craving all that his touch had once meant.

As though he'd been waiting for her gaze to lift to his, he smiled at her, a brilliant heart-tugging smile that mesmerised her into smiling back. And for that one incandescent moment, there was no darkness between them. None at all.

Then he turned to face the crowd and began to speak.

"Ladies and gentlemen..."

CHAPTER SIXTEEN

SHONTELLE hoarded that one lovely moment with Luis in her heart as she looked out at the elite gathering in front of them—*the ladies and gentlemen*—Elvira's guests, people who were important to the smooth running of Martinez interests, people of influence, people who mattered if Luis was to hold his stake in the family company. Their faces seemed to run together in a stream of avid curiosity.

She heard Luis take a deep breath before continuing, and tension screamed along her nerves again. Had he listened to her? Enough to put aside whatever plan he had to even the score for treating her badly? She didn't want some public humbling. She'd hate it. Please…let him satisfy these people and be content with his stand for personal integrity, she prayed with desperate fervour.

His deep, resonant voice seemed to boom through the ballroom. "…I am very proud to introduce to you, a woman of great heart and courage, Miss Shontelle Wright…"

Shontelle squirmed inside at the heightened interest he was stirring…spotlighting her. What was the point?

"Her brother, Alan, is a long-time friend of mine,"

Luis went on. "He worked with me at the Martinez mine in Brazil and has since built up a highly successful business, running tours of South America, using Buenos Aires as his base city." He gestured encouragement for approval as he added, "And, coincidentally, bringing a lot of tourist money into our country."

There was a buzz of appreciation from the spectators. Shontelle relaxed a little. She could see the need to publicly explain her connection to him.

"Last night, Shontelle braved breaking the curfew in La Paz to acquire a bus for Alan's tour group, some of whom were suffering seriously from altitude sickness."

The sympathetic murmurs around the ballroom did not soothe the alarm jabbing through Shontelle's mind. Luis wasn't going to reveal personal details, was he? She darted a sharp glance at him, eloquently appealing for discretion.

He smiled as though sharing something good with her, with everyone. "Today," he said, giving a timeframe which relieved her of her worst fears, "this amazingly resourceful lady saved me from one of the military tanks cruising the streets, just as I was looking straight down its gun barrel. Her beautiful fair hair provided the right distraction."

His blatantly admiring comments evoked a lighter humour in the crowd. There was a ripple of laughter as people visualised the scene he'd drawn for them.

Luis' smile widened to a grin. "I returned the favour later by jumping our bus over a trench which the farmers had dug across the road. It was a rather bumpy ride, but we survived it.''

Outright laughter, this time, and a burst of applause for their daring in getting out of La Paz. Shontelle found herself smiling, glad that Luis was turning what had been a nightmare into a tale to be enjoyed by others. It also neatly covered why they were together tonight, making his partnering her perfectly acceptable in the light of today's events.

The noise died down, the desire to hear more rising uppermost. Again Shontelle glanced at Luis, wondering where he would take them next. His expression had sobered. When he resumed speaking it was in a quieter, more confidential tone.

''I am happy to say there was more than survival involved in our long journey here to be with you tonight.''

He paused, galvanising everyone's attention.

''Two years ago, because of difficult, personal circumstances, Shontelle decided, much against my wishes, that she could not share her life with me.''

Oh, my God! He couldn't…he just couldn't reveal his mother's and Claudia's scheming in public! Shontelle could feel all her insides knotting up.

''Today, when both our lives were in danger, those circumstances no longer held any meaning,'' he went on.

How could he say that? Shontelle thought frantically. Their whole purpose here was to exact justice for those *circumstances!* And they'd done it. So what was he leading to now?

In sheer agitation she scraped her nails against his palm. He threaded his fingers through hers and gripped more tightly. It increased her agitation a hundredfold. She didn't know what he was tying her to.

He turned to look at her and all she could think of was...dark Angel...dark Angel... She sensed him reaching out through some critical mass, unsure of his way but bent on fighting every obstacle and suddenly the words he had spoken this morning burst into her mind—*for you I risk my life*—and she wanted to scream... *No!*...but her throat was too constricted to utter anything.

Then he spoke.

"To all of you I announce...this is the woman I love...and will always love."

The words vibrated through her, creating chaos. Impossible to sort out truth from need—either his or hers. Tears misted her eyes. She couldn't even see him clearly, let alone perceive what he meant by this public announcement.

"Shontelle..." His voice was husky. He poured more strength into it. "...Will you do me the honour of marrying me?"

Understanding came in a burst of anguish... *marriage or nothing.*

This was his offer...in atonement for last night...perhaps even in atonement for never having made their love public when it would have counted.

She wasn't *foreign trash* to him. He had paraded her as his partner into the highest of Martinez circles. Now he was offering her his name in front of these people...if she wanted it. And if she didn't...if she refused it publicly...he was prepared to have his pride sacrificed, just to give her the satisfaction of knowing he had paid her the highest compliment he could pay any woman.

To lay himself on the line like this...risking everything...as she had done last night, though differently, privately...was it an expression of abiding love...or an extreme expression of balancing the scales?

Panic coursed through her. He was waiting for her answer. Everyone was waiting. But the answer wasn't simple. Except...she was utterly incapable of humiliating Luis in front of these people. So there was no choice. And she had to speak.

"I..." Her mouth was hopelessly dry. Perversely, her eyes were awash with tears. She nodded to Luis as she tried to work moisture around her tongue, signalling the consent he had to want, for whatever reason he wanted it. Then in an explosive rush, she said what she had to say. "Yes, I will." Somehow it didn't seem enough, coming belatedly, so she quickly added, "I will marry you, Luis."

The words carried through the microphone for everyone to hear and they seemed to echo and echo, haunting her, until someone started clapping. The sound came from the side of the stage where they'd left Patricio and Elvira. Impossible to know who it was, slapping their palms in approval, but the action caught on and was repeated by others, more and more, building such a momentum, the ballroom seemed to thunder with the noise.

Luis released her hand and curved his arm around her shoulders, hugging her closely to him. Shontelle concentrated fiercely on blinking back tears, pasting a smile on her face. Unbelievably, she was being approved as Luis' wife-to-be and she still had to do him proud, regardless of her own tearing confusion.

"Gracias. Muchas gracias."

Maybe it was a distortion of the microphone but Luis' voice sounded thick with emotion. Shontelle reasoned it was huge relief that his public proposal had produced this result. Even she was stunned by this overwhelming acceptance of his choice. Was he a popular personage in Buenos Aires? Or had his presentation of a crossed love, revived in the face of possible death, struck some deep appeal?

Romance...

A fairy tale...

Cinderella claimed by the prince.

She was getting light-headed again, her mind dizzied by too many whirling thoughts. It was just as well Luis was holding her because her knees were trembling.

"In the hope..." he started again when the prolonged applause died down. "In my quite desperate hope...that Shontelle would agree to sharing her life with me..."

There was so much warm pleasure in his tone, Shontelle couldn't stop her heart from going mushy. If he really meant what he was saying...but what of his promise to have her at the airport tomorrow? How did that gell with this?

"...When we stopped on the road at Villa Tunari, this afternoon, I called ahead to Santa Cruz. As you know, Bolivia produces some of the finest emeralds in the world and there are some very fine jewellers in Santa Cruz. I wanted to present Shontelle with a ring tonight, an emerald to match her eyes."

He had been planning this...all those hours ago? From the moment she had agreed to accompany him to this reception? Shontelle's mind boggled. He'd been so...so businesslike in getting them here.

"So I had a selection brought to the airport..."

The attaché case!

"...And while Shontelle slept on the flight to Buenos Aires, I chose the one I now give her, as a token of my love, my commitment to her, and my belief in our future together."

Luis thrust the microphone into her right hand. In a helpless daze Shontelle watched him take the ring from his coat pocket, pick up her left hand, and slide onto the third finger the most amazing ring she'd ever seen—huge glittering emerald, set amongst an abstract cluster of baguette diamonds—like a perfect green pool surrounded by a pile of irregular rocks.

It won't fit, she thought wildly, but somehow it did, as though her finger had been measured for it. And it looked...totally incredible. She was still staring down at it—a fortune of precious stones displayed on her hand—on her engagement finger!—as Luis took the microphone again.

"I think I have surprised her," he said with such happy humour, people laughed indulgently.

Surprise was not the word for it, Shontelle thought, trying to struggle through a maze of shockingly unanswered questions.

"Since most of you have not yet met my wife-to-be," Luis raved on, "may I inform you Shontelle speaks fluent Spanish, probably knows more about our country than we do, and can dance a superb tango. Which I feel in the mood to demonstrate right now."

He waved to the orchestra to take their places on the stage in readiness, then appealed to the guests who were obviously enjoying his showmanship. "I invite you all to join us on the dance floor in celebration of a night to remember."

So now the tango, Shontelle thought, feeling helplessly entangled by decisions she had no hand in making. As Luis set the microphone back on its stand—the microphone that had made his proposal so terribly public—it struck Shontelle that he'd used it to virtually blackmail her.

Forcing his will?

Was this engagement really, truly what he wanted?

Nothing to do with justice?

Luis turned to her, his face alight with the exhilaration of having carried all before him, his eyes sparkling and his mouth almost dancing with a smile of wicked pleasure. He lifted her newly beringed hand to his lips, gave it a cavalier kiss, then slid his arm around her waist and swept her off the stage and onto the dance floor.

They were still very much on show, the guests

waiting for them to lead off, or watching to see if Shontelle could, indeed, dance a superb tango. Luis certainly exuded confidence as they positioned themselves in front of each other. Shontelle's heart was hammering, confusion still rife in her mind, but pride demanded she perform with all the skill she could muster, which meant she had to get her jelly-like legs in strong, agile order very fast.

It helped when she and Luis lifted their arms and settled into the initial embrace. Somehow his confidence flowed into her and his sheer arrogance in staging all this, sparked a gush of volatile energy. He might be the leader, she the follower in the sophisticated interrelation of steps in this dance, but the urge to challenge him with a few intricate improvisations of her own, tripping up his comfort zone, was very, very tempting.

The orchestra had chosen a 1950's song, setting a distinctive style and mood with its dramatic passion, which suited Shontelle's need for a little individual creativity. Luis had had a fine time manipulating her movements. He deserved to be pushed into meeting her initiatives.

"Just remember this dress doesn't have the mobility of a slit up the side," she warned him.

He laughed, his eyes very hotly wicked. "My control will be masterly."

It was a goad that fired Shontelle's blood. Luis Angel Martinez had taken far too much control upon himself. It was time to show him she had rights, too, including the right not to be boxed into a corner.

"Ready?" he asked with a cock of his eyebrow.

"*You* had better be...this time," she retorted with a mocking little smile.

He grinned and started them into the traditional *salida,* the basic walking pattern. Shontelle gave him his head for a while, following his perfectly executed figure eights, turns, twists, sweeps, but after he threw in a masterful drag, making himself very much the leader with her trailing in a feet-together slide, she started challenging him with subtle little embellishments to the hooks and kicks, forcing him into very fancy footwalk.

He growled at her, his eyes taking on a very animal gleam as he engineered a *sandwich,* catching her thigh against his, leaning into her, arching her back, his arm circling her so his hand was virtually cupping the underswell of her breast.

"Taking again, Luis?" Shontelle fired, seizing the advantage of close range.

"Giving. Giving with all I've got," he answered, and the raw desire in his eyes had nothing to do with justice.

He really did want her!
Still!
Maybe always?

Excitement sizzled through Shontelle.

The controlled elegance of their tango swiftly acquired a slinky sexuality, a stalking sexuality, and Shontelle deliberately kept it simmering with artfully provocative wiggles and shakes.

No point in pretending she didn't want him. He had a lot of answering to do, but if this night could lead to sharing their lives in an acceptable way, Shontelle was not going to turn her back on the possibility.

Luis swept her into double-time steps, moving into a high lift and a dexterous curl around him, re-establishing his dominance. She countered with a full body downward slide that left her in no doubt of his state of excitement.

They indulged themselves in the dramatic rhythm of the music, communicating heat that became so steamy, Shontelle felt herself in danger of melting on the floor. Only the wild exultation of more than matching Luis kept her feet twinkling, her body sensuously supple, and her head proudly held.

They were breathing hard when the music ended, her breasts heaving against his chest, their lower bodies entwined in the traditional aggressive/resistant pose, her arms held back, hair still swinging, and Luis' face hovering over hers.

But this wasn't the end, Shontelle thought in wild elation. Not in Luis' eyes. And the hopes that had seemed so foolish, danced their own irrepressible tango through her heart.

CHAPTER SEVENTEEN

HAD he done enough?

The question gnawed at Luis' mind as he watched Shontelle dancing with Patricio—a waltz, not the tango. No way would he allow any other man to dance the tango with her. A waltz was bearable...just. He itched to have her in his arms—only his—though he knew it was appropriate she dance with his brother; obvious evidence of family support, reinforcement of approval.

His plan had worked...so far. Shontelle was still carrying through the role he'd thrust upon her, but what she was feeling...what she was thinking...he couldn't even begin to be sure of that until this reception was behind them. The words she'd spoken during the tango kept haunting him—*Taking again, Luis?* Could his giving tonight make up for the way he'd treated her in La Paz? Was it enough?

He had done all he could here, Luis decided. His need to have Shontelle to himself could no longer be suppressed. He had to know if she'd been co-operating with everything for his sake—saving him from social disaster—or giving him the chance to show he meant what he said. If it was the latter case, there was hope.

A check of his watch showed it was close to three o'clock, not too early to leave.

"Impatient, Luis?" one of his friends asked, a knowing grin on his face.

"Who could blame him?" another remarked. "Such a woman would heat any man's veins. She is magnificent, Luis."

"She is, indeed," he agreed, smiling to cover his gut-twisting need to keep her in his life.

He signalled to one of the household staff and requested a message be immediately taken to Carlos—their car and driver to be summoned and waiting at the door for them.

Most of the guests looked set to party on and might well remain until dawn, but Luis had no doubt that indulgent understanding for his and Shontelle's early departure would be readily given. After all, it had been a long and highly eventful day and they had clearly won the popular vote tonight. Benevolence was still running strongly.

The Gallardo family had effected a tactful exit during the past hour, Esteban undoubtedly exercising his patriarchal authority to ensure there was no open rift between the families. If there was any accounting to be done, it would be done in boardrooms, not here. Saving face was just as important as holding profitable business connections. Luis had banked on that. Esteban Gallardo was a very pragmatic man.

Shontelle could no longer harbour any fear of being ostracised or snubbed by Argentinian society. On the contrary, over the past few hours, she had been showered with admiration and genuine good wishes. At least this much had been achieved, Luis thought with satisfaction.

The public response to *his* announcement had been all he could have wished. Not that it had been critically important, but it was helpful—one less issue to argue, once he and Shontelle were alone. *If* they got as far as argument.

Her acceptance of his proposal had been so long in coming, he certainly couldn't count on its lasting beyond the doors of this house. She'd promised support and she'd given it, right down the line. Though he'd felt there'd been more than support in the fire of her tango dancing. Surely she couldn't have been quite so excitingly sensual if she felt no desire for him. Unless it had been an angry tease.

Yet if she was nursing anger, there'd been no hint of it since then. She'd been warmly gracious through all the introductions, her apparent ease in bantering with him, smiling, laughing, giving him every encouragement to believe their partnership was real. Or was she simply acting out what she thought he expected of her?

It was possible her manner stemmed from a need to prove herself a match for him, whether she saw any future in it or not, but Luis fervently hoped it was motivated by more than personal pride.

The waltz ended.

Luis moved aside from his friends, compelled by

the urge to gather Shontelle to himself as soon as Patricio escorted her from the dance floor. *Magnificent* was an apt description, he thought, watching her walk towards him, the red and silver dress enhancing her glorious femininity, her hair flowing like a river of light, her face alive with vibrant personality. Everything she was called to him...body and soul, and the primitive caveman inside him was severely testing his control.

I have to win...

The thought—the need—burned through his mind, through his entire body. He held out his hand to her. Without hesitation she placed hers in it, though she bestowed her smile on his brother, making Luis' stomach clench with uncertainty.

"*Gracias,* Patricio," she said huskily.

"We'll leave now," Luis announced, the inner caveman insisting on it. He couldn't share any part of her with anyone anymore, not even his brother. "I appreciate your support, Patricio," he forced himself to add, sincerely grateful for his brother's stalwart defence of both their positions.

Patricio's eyes twinkled with understanding. "I could do with more warning next time you're intent on bearding lions, Luis. Though I must concede you do it with style." He lifted Shontelle's left hand, which he'd retained while they spoke, and bowed over it with excessive gallantry. "Forgive my trepidations, Shontelle. I am truly delighted to welcome you into the family. You do my brother proud."

"It's kind of you to say so," she replied, leaving Luis acutely aware there was no commitment in those words.

Having finally released Shontelle, Patricio gave Luis an earnest look. "Don't go without speaking to our mother. It was she who began the applause after Shontelle accepted your proposal of marriage."

It surprised him. "I thought it was you."

"I very quickly joined in but she led."

"Face saving," Luis interpreted sardonically.

Patricio shrugged. "A public step into your camp. It could mean more than you think."

"We shall see," Luis said noncommittally. "Goodnight, Patricio."

"Buenos noches."

Luis waved to the friends he'd been waiting with while Shontelle danced, then drew her down the ballroom towards the exit to the gallery, mentally crossing off another confrontation with his mother. Why risk her saying something unpalatable to Shontelle? He needed every advantage on his side.

"I take it *court is adjourned,*" Shontelle remarked dryly.

His heart contracted. Had it all been an act on her part? "I hope you feel justice has been done," he answered, willing her to look directly at him.

She flicked him a derisive glance. "It could have been a bit tricky there, if you'd produced a yellow diamond."

Tricky…yes, she could certainly accuse him of that.

Though, to him it had been a gamble, pure and simple. The biggest gamble of his life. And still he didn't know if the outcome was positive.

"Was an emerald the right choice for you?" he asked, almost begging for a hint.

Her mouth curved as she lifted her left hand and gazed down at the ring he'd put on her finger. "It's a very extravagant gesture, Luis," she said with a wry twist. "And it certainly served to persuade everyone you meant what you said."

She didn't believe him.

Shock rattled his confidence. What more could he do or say? Had his plan been futile from the start? *¡Dios!* He ached for her. He could not let her go. Frantically he counted the hours before he had to take her to the airport. Thirteen. Another two before the flight boarded. He had to make every minute work for him.

"I do mean it, Shontelle," he stated quietly. "I thought it was the only way to prove you could trust my word. In the circumstances…it seemed to me that actions would be more convincing than speech."

He felt the fingers that had been resting lightly within his grasp, curl into her palm with knuckle-tight intensity. Her left hand dropped to her side. Her head lowered. Shutting herself off from him, Luis thought, and frenziedly searched for some opening which might turn her towards him.

His mother intercepted their path to the gallery.

He silently cursed her interference. If she'd kept out of their lives two years ago...

"Luis, Shontelle...are you leaving?"

"I trust you're not going to stand in our way," he answered tersely, in no mood for political appeasement.

Her eyes looked sick, her face strained, yet neither sign of stress touched him. The damage she'd done went too deep. She touched his arm, a tentative reaching out which was uncharacteristic of her. Still he could not respond to the gesture. Two years...two years of being twisted around at her behest, and if he lost Shontelle now...

"I'm sorry. I was wrong," she acknowledged, her gaze sliding to Shontelle in bleak appeal, finding no softening in his for the admission that had been wrung out of her. "Shontelle, I beg you...don't take Luis from me."

Shades of Eduardo... Luis gritted his teeth against a savage wave of resentment. Couldn't his mother comprehend his need to be free of that blight on her life?

"I would never have done that, Señora Martinez. Nor will I now," Shontelle answered gently.

No, she would just walk away and leave him, as she had before, Luis thought bitterly.

"You...shame me."

Such humbling made him restive. He stared at his mother, unsure if this was some ploy to regain favour or a genuine expression of regret. Her face looked older, seamed with lines he hadn't noticed before—tired, sagging lines. It struck him forcefully that the indomitable arrogance was gone.

"I hope you can find it in your heart to forgive me...in time," she said haltingly, as though treading an unfamiliar path where the end could not be seen.

"Patricio said you started the clapping after I accepted Luis' proposal," Shontelle said with a slightly quizzical air.

Ascertaining the truth? Luis wondered. Why would it matter, if she didn't care?

"It was...something I could do," came the rueful reply. "I didn't know...no, I didn't allow myself to think...that Luis would...or could...love you so much." She looked back at him, openly pleading his forgiveness. "Please believe now...I wish you both...every happiness."

Virtually against his will, Luis found himself moved. Maybe an understanding could be reached with his mother if she was finally comprehending he was not her tool.

"Thank you," Shontelle murmured.

Polite to the end?

Luis tried to shake off the doubts plaguing him. "We'll talk...another time," he promised brusquely. "If you'll excuse us now?"

Elvira Rosa Martinez re-emerged. She nodded graciously and moved aside.

"Call Patricio to her, Luis," Shontelle whispered.

He frowned at her, hope warring with disbelief. Her

beautiful green eyes were filled with caring—sympathy, the wish to make things better. It stunned him.

"Now. Before we leave. Please?" she urged.

He looked back to where they'd left Patricio and found him watching them. Luis nodded towards his mother. It was enough. His brother raised a hand in a salute of understanding and started walking.

He met the query in Shontelle's eyes with a crooked little smile. "Done," he assured her.

His smile was returned. "She *is* your mother."

"And you? Are you my fiancée, Shontelle?"

Her lashes fluttered down. The slight curve of her lips disappeared as she sighed.

Luis held his breath.

"Let's get out of here, Luis."

It wasn't a no!

"I've already ordered the car. It should be waiting at the door."

She slid him an ironic look. "So efficient."

He laughed out of sheer relief that she hadn't handed him an outright rejection. Then he tucked her arm around his and swept her out of the ballroom, a full complement of newly vitalised energy coursing through him.

The reception had served its purpose.

Shontelle *wanted* to be alone with him.

He had thirteen hours to win her over.

CHAPTER EIGHTEEN

FIVE more minutes, Luis told himself as he settled into the car beside Shontelle. The desire to reach out and haul her onto his lap and hug her tightly to him, washing away whatever doubts she had with a passionate rain of kisses, was pumping through him. But *taking* might not be a good idea, particularly not in the car. The chauffeur would get them to his apartment soon enough. Then he wouldn't have to stop. Unless Shontelle...

He took a deep breath and looked at her, craving some sign that she felt the same urgent desire for him. Her gaze was turned back at the house, remaining fixed on it even as the chauffeur drove towards the exit gates. Worried that the whole wretched Martinez heritage it represented might still be a barrier between them, and determined on smashing all barriers, Luis seized Shontelle's hand to draw her attention to him.

Her head snapped around, her eyes meeting his, but with a faraway look in them that screwed up his gut again. His fingers dragged over her palm, the need to get under her skin burning through him. Her expression changed, inviting him into the rueful reflection in her mind.

"We've never had a tragedy in our family, Luis.

I'm sorry I didn't understand…didn't appreciate the toll it can take." She squeezed his hand. "However hard it was, I'm glad it was faced tonight. I think it was good for all of you. And for me. It showed me things aren't always what they seem on the surface."

Relief surged through him. There was nothing negative in that little speech. "What things?" he prompted.

She shrugged. "I put your mother's rejection of me down to snobbery and I didn't think that would change. But it wasn't snobbery. It went much deeper…"

"It had to do with power, Shontelle," he supplied.

She nodded. "Yes, I see that now." Her eyes searched his in anxious concern. "Will there be a backlash from the Gallardo family?"

"I doubt it. In any case, there's little they can do to really hurt the Martinez company. It's not vulnerable to attack. There could be deals that won't now be made, but overall, it's not a make or break situation."

With a satisfied sigh, she looked down at her lap where her left hand rested. Even in the dimness of the car the emerald and diamond ring glittered as she stretched out her fingers, apparently studying his gift to her.

Once again Luis was racked with uncertainty. Had he chosen wrongly? Was she preparing to take it off and return it to him?

"I thought…last night…it was all gone…what

there'd been between us,'' she said quietly, still gazing down at the ring as though unsure whether to believe what it stood for.

He winced, fiercely wishing he could turn back the clock and do it all differently. She might have told him the truth last night if he'd given her any leeway, shown her…what? His love for her had been buried under so much bitter fury and frustration, there was no way it could have been expressed. So why should she believe him now?

Despairingly he sought for an answer she might accept. His mind was a blank. The urge to just pull her into his arms was barely containable. Words were no good. He had to show her…make her feel all the positive flow inside him. Not like last night. Completely different.

''You'd better tell me,'' she went on, catching back his attention, pausing the wild train of thought. ''Was tonight…'' She hesitated. The corner of her mouth turned down into a grimace. ''Well, it served many purposes, didn't it?''

''No.'' The word burst from him with passionate vehemence, the built-up tension reaching breaking point. ''*¡Dios!* Look at me!''

She did, her eyes wide and questing and seemingly reflecting his own desperate need.

''I hated you last night, Shontelle. I hated you because for two damnably empty years I'd wanted and needed and craved the love I'd felt we'd shared. Then when I realised today we *did* share it…'' That dreadful moment of revelation rushed back on him, choking him momentarily. He swallowed hard and pushed out the truth. The only truth that counted. "I'd do anything to have it again. *Anything!* Do you understand?"

The car stopped.

Luis couldn't bear to wait another second. Shontelle was just staring at him in a kind of awed daze. He was out of the car and around it to her side before the chauffeur had alighted. He easily beat the man to opening Shontelle's door. Without a pause, he scooped her off the seat and swung her up against his chest, one arm under her knees, the other cradling her close, the caveman inside him rampaging straight through any other considerations...his woman, *his!*

"Don't say no!" he heard himself wildly muttering as he carried her to the door of his apartment.

Her warm breath fanned his ear as she wound her arms around his neck. "Can I touch you tonight?" she asked huskily.

"Yes," he hissed. "Touch me all you like. Anywhere. Everywhere."

"No holds barred?"

Was that a teasing note in her voice? He wasn't sure. Didn't care. "None. None at all," he repeated gruffly. "Hang on to me. I've got to get the door key."

He felt like kicking the door in but some grain of sanity told him it was too solid. Shontelle didn't seem to mind him hoisting her over his shoulder as he fumbled in his pocket. She started to laugh. Laughter was good, wasn't it? His heart was thumping so hard he could hardly put two thoughts together.

He jammed the key in the door and one more barrier gave way. They were inside. A satisfying kick closed out the rest of the world.

"Put me down, Luis," Shontelle said in a breathless gurgle.

"Soon." He charged for the bedroom.

"Not on the bed," she managed more emphatically.

"Not?" It seemed a very good place to him.

"On my feet. Now!" she commanded, wriggling to break his hold.

It was against every raging instinct, but...somehow he managed enough control to pull himself back from falling onto the bed with her. He set her on her feet, though it was quite impossible to pluck his hands away from her waist. A hold was a hold and releasing her altogether was unthinkable.

"I don't want you to tear my dress," she said.

"I'll get you another."

"No, this one is special. Put the light on, Luis."

"Light," he echoed, telling himself "special" was good. It was okay to let go. For a few seconds. He did it to switch on the light.

She was grinning at him, her beautiful green eyes sparkling, dancing, teasing with wicked delight. "It's my turn to undress you," she said pointedly. "All touching permitted."

And the driving urgency inside him shattered into a brilliant burst of happiness. It was all right. Just like it used to be between them. The freedom of it bubbled through him…glorious, exhilarating, exultant freedom.

"Yes," he said, and he knew her grin was on his face…exactly the same…sharing…no barriers, no inhibitions, nothing coming between them except clothes. "How about one each? My tie, your necklace, my coat, your dress…" He cocked an eyebrow at her. "It'll go much faster."

She laughed and started undoing his bow tie, her eyes flirting deliciously with his. "I don't want it to go fast, Luis. I want to revel in every moment."

And suddenly, so did he, though there was one thing he needed to hear. "You do still love me." It came out more a statement than a question because he just couldn't accept a question, not with her hands on him, the look in her eyes, the pleasure humming through him.

She sighed. "Looks like I'm stuck on you, for better or for worse. Which reminds me, naked is fine, but if you think you're going to get this ring off me…"

"I want you to say it, Shontelle," he cut in, the yearning to hear the words too needy for playfulness.

She slid his tie out from his collar, linked her hands around his neck and raised her lashes, revealing the windows to her soul. "I love you, Luis Angel

Martinez. There never has been anyone else for me. And never will be.''

She carried that promise on her lips to his and Luis' heart seemed to pump liquid fire through him as they kissed, and kissed, and kissed, hungry for the giving of each other, the knowing, the certainty, the lifting of every last shadow on a love that should never have been shadowed.

He was so beautiful...so intoxicatingly beautiful... the feel of him, the smell of him, the sight of him...Shontelle felt as though her whole body was effervescing with happiness, her skin tingling like champagne.

Her man...her mate in every sense there was... and when they did move to the bed, it was together...together in all the ways she had craved last night, the giving and taking so excitingly, blissfully mutual, the sheer ecstacy of loving and feeling herself loved, the intense pleasure of touching, not just physically, but knowing how deeply it went, the wonderful, awesome flow of becoming one again, one in heart and mind and soul.

It was so incredibly special...this filling of all the empty spaces that had blighted two years of their lives...the unanswered needs and desires and hopes and dreams. It was as though everything they'd felt for each other had been waiting, trapped in a time-warp, and the release of it was heaven.

And when he entered her, slowly, both of them

treasuring the magical sensation of ultimate intimacy, his face hovering above hers, their eyes mirroring the rapture they shared…that was heaven, too, and she heard it in his voice as he murmured, "Shontelle…" and tasted it in his mouth as he kissed her, making the melding complete, and in her mind beat the one beautiful word… Angel…Angel…Angel.

It was goodness and light and joy and it moved into a rhythm that celebrated the life they would have together. She wrapped her legs around him in exultant possession and lifted herself to him, urging the feast of sharing that would always be theirs…the feast of love…free to soar into any future they decided upon, because the form didn't matter. This was the substance of it, the essence of it, the fusion of their lives.

Then there was no thought…only feeling… powerful waves of feeling, obliterating everything but the sense of their oneness, peaking into a sublime climax, a pulsing flow that lingered on and on, permeating their embrace as they lay together in the harmony of utter fulfilment.

"Thank you," Luis whispered, his voice furred with deep emotion. "Thank you for being you and loving me."

"It was meant to be," she murmured, feeling that as a deep, unalterable truth. "I felt only half alive without you, Luis."

"And I without you." He raised himself up on his elbow to look into her eyes. His were dark velvet, glowing with lovely soft warmth. "Where would you like our future to be, Shontelle? If you want me to move to Australia…''

''No!'' She was shocked he would even think of it. ''Your life is here, Luis. I'm happy to be here with you.'' Besides, she had more or less promised his mother she wouldn't take Luis away. She couldn't compound the tragedy of Eduardo's loss by removing Luis from all Elvira held dear.

''Away from your family?'' he softly reminded her.

Shontelle hesitated a moment, knowing she would miss them, wishing they were not so far away. But by air it was only a day's travel. ''We could visit them, couldn't we?'' she appealed hopefully.

He smiled. ''As often as you like, my love. And, of course, I shall fly to Australia to meet your parents and discuss our marriage plans with them.''

''Okay, master planner,'' she happily teased. ''What is your schedule for that?''

He grinned. ''Well, since I have to put you on the plane with Alan all too soon…''

He intended to keep his promise, which was only right, but it gave them such little time together just now when…

''…I thought I could follow next week.''

Relief and pleasure instantly swamped the little jab of disappointment.

''Which gives you time to prepare your family,'' he went on purposefully, ''and me time to deal with mine.''

"I thought your mother was…well, accepting tonight," she reminded him.

He nodded. "I just want to make sure everything's ironed out before you come back with me."

She smiled, joy bubbling through her. "So you're flying out to Australia to fetch me, are you?"

His eyes sparkled. "One week alone I can manage. But only with the promise I don't have to spend any more of my life without being able to reaffirm this."

He kissed her, long and lovingly.

"I promise," she murmured, moving against him with languorous sensuality, happy to have absolutely everything reaffirmed as much and as often as Luis liked.

Which was how they spent the hours leading up to their departure for the airport, hours well used, deliciously used, and when they joined up with the tour group at the terminal, the glow of their love for each other was like a neon light to Alan and everyone else.

No one asked Shontelle to do anything. She and Luis were left alone to talk the talk of lovers soon to be separated, but knowing it wouldn't be for long. The promise was real, as real as the emerald and diamond ring on her finger, and every bit as lasting as all the precious stones in the world.

"One week," Luis said with passionate longing when he finally had to let her go to board the plane.

"I'll be waiting at Sydney airport for you," Shontelle promised.

"I'll call you every day," he vowed.

"Yes, yes."

She had to go. One quick last kiss and she ran to catch the others, her feet yearning to dance a wild and wonderful tango because she was coming back to Luis, coming back to Argentina, coming back to the love of a lifetime.

Nothing was banished forever.

Marriage was the final act.

CHAPTER NINETEEN

"I NOW declare you man and wife."

At last, Luis thought, a sense of triumph soaring through him. The commitment of marriage was sealed. Three months he'd waited for this, three months of wanting it every day, craving the security of knowing with absolute certainty that nothing could stop it. Now he could breathe easily. He and Shontelle were publicly, legally wed. Their future together was assured.

Brimming with elation, he turned to lift the veil from his bride's face. Shontelle's beautiful green eyes were shiny with tears, just as they'd been when he'd asked her to marry him in front of the very same people who now filled the church. But there was no doubting the emotion behind these tears.

Love...love and joy and sparkles of sheer blinding happiness.

"You may kiss the bride."

He took her in his arms. Heart of my heart, he thought, and kissed her, feeling a glorious sense of completion. Husband and wife—one in name—one in everything—and they would cherish each other for the rest of their lives, cherish all they were to each other.

181

"I love you, Shontelle," he whispered as he lifted his mouth from hers.

"I love you, Luis Angel Martinez," she answered with a wealth of feeling, rolling his name off her tongue as though it was the most magical name in the world.

"Well, *Señora* Martinez," he rolled back at her, grinning from ear to ear. "Ready to face the world as my wife?"

"Anytime," she declared, sharing his grin.

Anytime... It was music to his ears. Shontelle at his side, standing by him, right down the line. Faith, trust, love, loyalty, boundless support...he had no doubt she would give them unstintingly, just as he would to her. All that was needed was to be honest with each other and that lesson had been learnt. Too painfully to recollect it now. Today there was no pain and he fiercely hoped it was forever in the past.

This was the real beginning of their lives together.

As they turned for the walk down the aisle, he tucked her arm around his, feeling a huge surge of love and pride. Patricio and Alan ranged up beside him. Alan's wife, Vicki, and his own young cousin, Maria, fussed over the train of Shontelle's beautiful bridal gown.

His mother rose to her feet from the front pew, looking very much the impressive figure she'd always been. Luis still found it difficult to forgive the two years she'd taken from him and Shontelle.

You see? he beamed at her with all the positive

energy pulsing through his mind. This is right. This is good. This is how it should be between a man and his woman.

She smiled and nodded, accepting his choice, and the scarring on his soul faded under a flow of contentment. He knew there would still be skirmishes over her way and his, but the war had been won. Elvira Rosa Martinez had conceded there was a power beyond her grasp. Wealth and influence could not buy love. He hoped she kept remembering that truth.

But it was irrelevant right now.

He and Shontelle were married.

Irrevocably married.

If problems arose they'd work them out. If they had differences of opinion, they'd talk them through. Nothing was ever going to tear them apart again.

His gaze was drawn to her parents rising from their pew, their blessing having been given to this marriage without any reservation at all. Their daughter loved him. And he silently vowed to them he'd return her love a hundredfold.

The organ began to play, filling the church with its rich, resonant sound. Luis hugged Shontelle's arm closer to him and of one accord they stepped forward, heading down the aisle to the exultant lilt of the last piece of ceremonial music, heading towards the life they would forge together.

A shining future, Luis thought, watching Shontelle bestowing a brilliant smile on all the guests they passed. She dazzled them, just as she dazzled him...always had, always would.

With her there was no darkness.

She was the sun and the moon and the stars.

Shontelle...his wife.

He'd won.

They were married.

Luis Angel Martinez smiled, too.

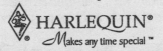

HARLEQUIN ◆ PRESENTS®

THE BARONS

One sister, three brothers— who will inherit, and will they all find lovers?

Jonas is approaching his eighty-fifth birthday, and he's decided it's time to choose the heir of his sprawling ranch, Espada. He has three ruggedly good-looking sons, Gage, Travis and Slade, and a beautiful stepdaughter, Caitlin.

Who will receive Baron's bequest? As the Baron brothers and their sister discover, there's more at stake than Espada. For love also has its part to play in deciding their futures....

Enjoy Gage's story:
Marriage on the Edge
Harlequin Presents #2027, May 1999

And in August, get to know Travis a whole lot better in
More than a Mistress
Harlequin Presents #2045

Available wherever Harlequin books are sold.

HARLEQUIN®
Makes any time special ™

EXPECTING

She's sexy, she's successful... and she's pregnant!

Relax and enjoy these new stories about spirited women and gorgeous men, whose passion results in pregnancies... sometimes unexpectedly! All the new parents-to-be will discover that the business of making babies brings with it the most special love of all....

Harlequin Presents® brings you one **EXPECTING!** book each month throughout 1999.
Look out for:

The Unexpected Father by Kathryn Ross
Harlequin Presents® #2022, April 1999

The Playboy's Baby by Mary Lyons
Harlequin Presents® #2028, May 1999

Accidental Baby by Kim Lawrence
Harlequin Presents® #2034, June 1999

The Unexpected Baby by Diana Hamilton
Harlequin Presents® #2040, July 1999

Available wherever Harlequin books are sold.

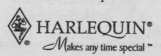

HARLEQUIN®
Makes any time special ™

Coming Next Month

HARLEQUIN PRESENTS®

THE BEST HAS JUST GOTTEN BETTER!

#2043 TO BE A HUSBAND Carole Mortimer
Bachelor Brothers
It's the first time for Jonathan that any woman has resisted his charm. What does he have to do to win over the cool, elegant Gaye Royal? Propose marriage? But being a husband is the last thing Jonathan has in mind....

#2044 THE WEDDING-NIGHT AFFAIR Miranda Lee
Society Weddings
As a top wedding coordinator, Fiona was now organizing her ex-husband's marriage. But Philip wasn't about to let their passionate past rest. Then Fiona realized that Philip's bride-to-be didn't love him...but Fiona still did!

#2045 MORE THAN A MISTRESS Sandra Marton
The Barons
When Alexandra Thorpe won the eligible Travis Baron for the weekend, she didn't claim her prize. Travis is intrigued to discover why the cool blond beauty had staked hundreds of dollars on him and then just walked away....

#2046 HOT SURRENDER Charlotte Lamb
Zoe was enraged by Connel's barefaced cheek! But he had the monopoly on sex appeal, and her feelings had become so intense that Zoe couldn't handle him in her life. But Connel always got what he wanted: her hot surrender!

#2047 THE BRIDE'S SECRET Helen Brooks
Two years ago, Marianne had left her fiancé, Hudson de Sance, in order to protect him from a blackmailer. But what would happen now Hudson had found her again, and was still determined to marry her?

#2048 THE BABY VERDICT Cathy Williams
Jessica was flattered when Bruno Carr wanted her as his new secretary. She hadn't bargained on falling for him—or finding herself pregnant with his child. Bruno had only one solution: marriage!